THE VOICES OF SILENCE

Bel Mooney studied English at University College London and then embarked upon a successful career in journalism that now spans four decades. In addition to making many programmes for radio and television, she has contributed to most national newspapers, notably *The Times*, the *Sunday Times* and the *Mirror*. Currently Bel is a travel writer and book critic for *The Times* as well as writing a highly respected column on human relationships for the *Daily Mail*. She is also the author of a number of fiction and non-fiction titles for both adults and children and is well known for her hugely popular Kitty series for younger readers.

Bel lives in Bath with her husband and a small white dog called Bonnie, who will soon be starring in her very own series. You can find out more about Bel and her books at:

www.belmooney.co.uk

For Robin

This is a work of fiction. Names, characters, places and incidents are
either the product of the author's imagination or, if real, are used fictitiously.

First published in Great Britain 1994 by Methuen Children's Books Ltd

This edition published 2007 by Walker Books Ltd
87 Vauxhall Walk, London SE11 5HJ

2 4 6 8 10 9 7 5 3 1

© 1994 Bel Mooney

Background cover photograph: Mihai E. Popa

The right of Bel Mooney to be identified as author of this work
has been asserted by her in accordance with the
Copyright, Designs and Patents Act 1988

This book has been typeset in M Joanna

Printed in Great Britain by J. H. Haynes & Co. Ltd

British Library Cataloguing in Publication Data:
a catalogue record for this book is available from the British Library

ISBN 978-1-4063-0727-6

www.walkerbooks.co.uk

The Voices of Silence

Bel Mooney

WALKER
BOOKS

ONE

When I was a little girl I actually used to dream of it. I would be in a boat, gliding through sparkling water, and there in the distance I'd see an island. But it wasn't green like real islands are. It was all dark brown, as if someone had lit a fire and burnt up the whole place. But of course, I knew differently. And as my boat came nearer I grew more and more excited, until at last, with only a few yards to go, I couldn't wait any longer. So I'd leap out, feel the water cool on my skin, wade forward, then throw myself on the ground and scoop up the brown pebbles on the beach, cramming them into my mouth.

Only they weren't pebbles, of course.

Chocolate.

The whole island was made of chocolate.

That was what I dreamt of, when I was a little girl. It was much better than a gingerbread house, because there was no wicked witch on my island; there was nobody but me. And in the silence, the absolute silence, I could eat and eat, and never feel sick. Later I'd change the dream so that there was a banana tree in the middle of the island as well. Chocolate and bananas ... and not have to share with a soul. I knew what paradise meant, even if only in my dreams.

I once asked the little boy on the floor below what he wanted for Christmas. He pursed his lips and frowned, and thought for a long time. Then a big smile crossed his face, and his eyes shone and he said, "A BANANA!" Despite my own fantasies I thought it a strange thing for a seven-year-old boy to want for his "big" present: not a car or a train but a banana!

"Why don't we have things like bananas, Mama?" I asked.

She shook her head sadly.

"How can I begin to start to tell you, Flora?" she said. "We just aren't so lucky — as some countries."

"You should answer the child's questions properly," muttered my father.

She shook her head, giving him one of those warning looks I had just started to notice.

"You should know better, Constantin," said Mama.

"Tell me, Tata," I said.

"We don't have chocolate, or bananas – or cheese or butter or meat, or even fresh bread for that matter – because we're lucky enough to live in the glorious Socialist Republic of Romania, watched over by our magnificent leader Comrade Ceauşescu. He knows it would be bad for our souls to be corrupted by the disgusting luxuries they enjoy in America, Britain, France and Germany. So that's it, little Flora."

All that came out in a quiet burst, as if he wanted to throw back his head and yell, and yet was being pressed down by something unseen, so that the words escaped like steam from under a lid. And Mama shook her head furiously, and said "Shhhh!"

That was a couple of years ago, and then I began to notice the "SHHHHHHHs" more and more. All questions silenced. Yet I wanted to talk. I *needed* to talk. Maybe that was one of the things that led me astray... Oh, but that's to jump ahead. And I must tell my story just as it happened.

It all began the day my best friend and I had an argument – one of those silly quarrels over nothing which end up by changing things for ever.

Alys and I live in neighbouring blocks on an estate in Bucharest. Four massive blocks, each twenty stories high – that's all. I've seen pictures of other places, of rolling green fields, grand houses, pretty cottages, and wide white sands under vivid blue skies, and huts on stilts. So I know that where we live is ugly and mean. Tata says it stops your spirit from growing, living in a place like this.

Every morning I run down the stairs from the tenth floor (they were going to build lifts – the shafts are there, all boarded up because the money ran out), and go outside to the stretch of rough ground between the blocks and wait for Alys. Sometimes she is there already, with her bag hitched on her shoulder, and her big grin. Usually we don't speak much. We just walk to school together, just as we always have.

When we were smaller we'd sometimes race, especially if it was raining. Alys might challenge me to jump one of the huge puddles which collect in the unfinished ground, and stay long after the sun had come out. But we don't race or jump any more, because it's childish. To be quite honest, I stopped it anyway because Alys always beat me. I am small and thin and not good at any games, whereas Alys is taller and very strong, and brilliant at running, all sports, and gym. People say she will be a great athlete one day. Sometimes that really annoys me.

(Before I go on, I have to be really honest. I was only just starting to realize that it was possible to love someone and resent her at the same time, so that sometimes the two feelings fight such a battle inside you, it leaves you breathless. Sometimes you even want the person you love to go far away, just so you'll be spared the turmoil. I was starting to feel like that about Alys. To me she was a perfect person: tall, slim, pretty, with blonde hair that curled round her face. She was clever in class, as well as good at sport, and to make it even worse, the kind of smiling person everyone likes; whilst I had started peering into the awful foggy mirror in our tiny bathroom, and saw this plain, spotty, cross, person, with dark hair that always looks lank no matter how much I stick it under the kitchen tap. So I could hate Alys Grosu, even though I looked forward to seeing her every day.)

"There's going to be a new boy in class today," Alys said as we drew near the school gates, streaming in with hundreds of others, all dressed alike in dark clothes.

"Who told you?" I asked.

"I heard the old Monster talking to one of the other teachers."

"Listening at doors, Alys! You'll get reported," I teased.

She laughed. "Who by – you?"

"Don't say that. It's not something to joke about."

"Rubbish! As far as I'm concerned you can make jokes about anything and everything," said

Alys gaily; then dropped her voice to a silly stage whisper and added, "even old Ceauşescu."

"Shhhh!" I went, and looked over my shoulder quickly.

The boy was just a few yards behind us, but didn't look as if he had heard. I just knew right away he must be the new boy. He was walking confidently and looked somehow different to all the pupils crowding round him.

I turned back quickly, but not before he had caught my gaze and nodded coolly in my direction. I felt my face grow hot. I nudged Alys sharply.

"Look behind … oh, not so obviously, you fool!"

"Mmm, if that's the new boy, he's quite an addition," she grinned. "He looks like a … a film star."

"You've never seen a film star," I muttered.

"How do you know what goes on in my dreams?" she retorted.

I looked around again, trying to be subtle – but he had gone.

In class we went through all the usual stuff: chanting out our loyalty to Romania, and to our beloved President, Nicolae Ceauşescu. By now I had stopped thinking about the words. Once, when I was younger, I started to sing a song at home, which we had learnt in the Young Pioneers – all about how Comrade Ceauşescu was our father and his wife Elena was our mother, and how their love for us shone like the sun. But Tata spoke sharply to me and told me to shut up. Now I just thought it was all rubbish and it didn't bother me.

Anyway, when all that was done the Monster told us to make Daniel Ghiban welcome, and then stopped the whispering and staring by bringing his hand sharply down on the table, and telling us to open our maths books. That was it for the rest of the morning, and I couldn't even twist round and see – because Ghiban had been put immediately behind me. Once or twice I glanced across to Alys and she raised her eyebrows, twitched her nose, and grinned knowingly. It made her look rather silly, I thought.

So I put everything out of my mind, and buried my nose in equations – thinking that there, at least, amongst the small letters and numbers, it was all right for meaning to be hidden, and for things to stand for something else.

I suppose you could say that my life, up to this point, had revolved around food, parents, food, Alys, school ... and food. Mama said it was the way I was built: thin and wiry like a little cat, and so always hungry. When you are little you don't

11

notice things: your mother getting up at 5 a.m. winter and summer alike, and going out into the chilly dawn to queue for bread and milk, and anything else she can find. And Tata would always carry an old shopping bag, sometimes getting home very late from the factory because, he said, he'd seen a queue and joined it, since it was bound to be something we needed. Some nights he'd come in with his face split in two with joy, holding the bag in the air like a trophy. And there would be a treat, like four or five apples, or some bacon, or a lump of cheese. Would we have a feast!

Then, later, you start to be aware – and you could kick yourself for the number of times you had whined about wanting milk or fruit, and your mother would slump wearily into the chair, as if it was all her fault. Which, of course, it was not.

So it isn't very surprising that my first impression of Daniel Ghiban was to do with food, even though other girls noticed his hair (dark and slicked back in a style we thought modern and daring) and his clothes (of which more later). But me – I noticed his food.

Everybody took a sandwich wrapped in brown paper for the middle of the day. Today mine was some fried onion between two thick slices of heavy white bread. All the kids had similar things – or maybe a slice of cold corn mush, making the paper wet and soggy. Unsurprisingly there was a small group of boys standing around Daniel Ghiban. They probably thought they were being friendly, but people aren't so friendly in our country; they're more curious, wanting to find out all they can. It was obvious, from the sudden burst of excited comment, that something unusual was happening. So Alys and I, with four or five other girls, moved in closer to see.

Meat!

He had real meat in his sandwich. And the bread was soft and fresh. *And* he had a piece of cake which looked delicious. My mouth began to water, and I looked down at what I had with distaste. I suppose that's the first time you let your parents down, when you feel ashamed of the best they can give.

We moved away again, the other girls chattering with excitement.

"Did you see that?"

"It looked like beef – lucky thing!"

"Never mind that – what about the *jeans!*"

"Real. Definitely real."

"Oh my God!"

"He's handsome – don't you think?"

"Think! Know, more likely."

"I wish he'd talk to me…"

"Definitely one hundred per cent."

"I bet he thinks he's wonderful," said Alys.

"Fancy having real meat in your sandwich," I said.

"I can't imagine," said Alys.

"Hey, Alys," said a girl called Adriana, who was jealous of Alys, "I bet, if you play it right, he'd give you a bite!"

With that the rest of them collapsed in silly giggles, and so we moved away disdainfully just as the buzzer went.

When the Monster gave us the result of the early morning maths test the new boy had got the highest mark, beating Alys. (I forgot to say she was usually top of the class in maths and science, although I could usually beat her in history and in composition.) I don't remember much about the rest of the day, until it was time to go home. We were surging out towards the cloakroom, when the handle on my bag broke suddenly (poor Mama had mended it about five times), and all my books cascaded to the floor. Alys had gone on ahead and didn't notice; those who were left laughed at me and walked on. I knelt down to start picking up the scattered work — when suddenly there was another pair of hands helping.

Daniel Ghiban.

"Don't worry about it," I muttered, feeling embarrassment flame in my cheeks.

"It's OK. I'll help," he said.

"Really, I'm fine," I said quickly as I stood up, clutching an assortment of books and papers to my chest.

"What about the one that got away?" he smiled, pointing at my pencil, which had rolled across the corridor.

He stepped across, bent down slowly, and picked it up. He was just in the process of handing it to me, with a flourish, when he glanced at it and frowned.

"Wait – it's broken."

"It's OK. Give it to me."

"Do you have a sharpener?"

"A what? Of course not. What's wrong with the kitchen knife?" I said.

"Just wait a moment," he said – and rummaged in his bag, before bringing out a smart plastic pencil case. "Look!"

Very carefully he sharpened my pencil with a beautiful metal pencil sharpener – the like of which I had never seen in my life. Then he handed it back to me with the warmest, friendliest smile so that I forgot to be cross or shy, and felt like the luckiest person in the world.

"Here you are... What's your name?"

"Popescu – Flora," I said.

"Borrow it whenever you like, Flora," he said casually, before hitching his bag on his shoulders and walking on.

I packed all my things back, clutched my own ruined bag to my chest, and walked to where Alys was waiting on the corner. She glanced at me curiously, and I could feel my smile lighting up the whole corridor. But I couldn't stop it. You know when a grin takes you over, as if your mouth is the open entrance to your whole soul?

We walked halfway home in silence. Then I said gloomily that I didn't know if my mother would be able to fix the wretched bag yet again, and what was I going to do? But Alys wasn't listening.

"So what do you think of him, then?" she asked.

"Who?" I asked, knowing perfectly well.

"The new boy."

"I think the same as everyone thinks," I said. "He's good-looking, got decent clothes, and is lucky enough to be given meat sandwiches. His Dad probably works for a butcher."

"I wonder where he's come from?" she said. "I mean, people don't move, do they?"

"Not usually," I said.

"Mmm," she said and suddenly I felt irritated.

"What do you mean, Mmm?" I asked.

"There's something about him I don't like," said Alys.

I thought of Daniel, and the way he was the only one who had stopped to help me, and how he'd done it in such a nice way, and bothered to sharpen my pencil for me, and how he was new anyway and so Alys didn't even know him.

"Probably the fact that he beat you in maths," I retorted.

"That's just silly," said Alys crossly.

"Well aren't you being silly?" I replied.

"No, I'm not," she said, in a distant, grown-up sort of way that made me feel crosser than ever.

"Yes you are," I said knowing how childish it sounded.

Alys shrugged. "Well, in that case we might as well stop talking!"

And a few minutes later she veered sharply away, not even saying goodbye, just doing her athletic loping run across the wasteland towards her block. Usually we stood and talked for a while, or even went to one or other of our flats for a short time – but not tonight. It left me feeling cold and lonely, as if Alys was a warm fire I was used to sitting by, that had suddenly been put out. But I couldn't understand who had done it. The sudden squabble had been so silly.

When I let myself into our flat I slumped in my usual chair by the dining table, feeling miserable. Nobody was in. Mama would arrive home from her museum job very soon, and Tata would get home from the factory about an hour after that. So there was nobody to tell.

In any case, what would I tell them?

Parents (I'd discovered) didn't understand about friendships, and how important it was to be liked by people your own age. Mama worried about food and life, and Tata muttered about life and politics, and both of them nagged me to work hard at school – even though (honestly) I couldn't see the point except if you could be really rich and get things like chocolate on the black market. People like my parents had gone to University, and worked hard, but they couldn't get decent jobs. So Tata was a factory worker, and Mama stood around in the National Museum all day, and we had no money. No wonder I escaped into my daydreams, and those lovely fairytales of Inspirescu. But Mama and Tata couldn't escape. They worried about *everything*. So what could I tell them? A quarrel with Alys? They'd think it unimportant. They wouldn't understand.

Sometimes that knowledge makes you lonelier

than ever, and you long to be a little child again, when your parents are the very centre of your whole universe, and you believe that they know the answers to everything and can make everything all right, always. When you get to be eleven or twelve you suddenly see it isn't true, and notice how your parents have as many faults as you do. Then all the safe, cosy walls around you crumble slowly down, and you have to step out over the debris into the cold wind, and find your way in this new country on your own.

After that, the worst thing is the responsibility.

You can't let them know that you know.

So I sat there at the table, looking around our tiny flat (only two rooms and a tiny kitchen and bathroom), and knowing that I'd have to pretend everything was all right. So I started by chucking all the things from my bag on to the sofa (which turned into their double bed at night) just to see if I could get some string and mend the handle on my own.

Then I stopped, and picked up the pencil with a point that was neater, more regular, more perfectly, *precisely* sharp than I had ever known – and looked at it carefully.

I pressed it against my palm.

Ow!

The sharp jab was real; the pencil was beautiful. It made me want to do my homework for once – and gave me some small consolation, because the new boy had said that I could borrow his sharpener whenever I wanted. He was friendly, and I wanted to forget all that stupid giggling about his hair, and his jeans, and the navy blue jumper with a badge on one side. Oh, and trainers, too – I forgot the trainers…

When I thought of his packed lunch I felt a pang of longing in my stomach as sharp as the pencil. And envy – real envy.

Anyway, none of that was important.

He had *talked* to *me*, that was what mattered. And that made me push aside my unhappiness at quarrelling with Alys. Alys had been mean and unfair about someone who was trying to be friendly. I had been right to snap back at her. It was, I decided, all her fault.

TWO

Just after that things started to happen at home which did push the business of Alys, and Daniel Ghiban, to the back of my mind. I became aware of an unusual atmosphere – a degree of silence between my parents which I could not understand. They had always been lively and talkative. Despite all our problems, and the anger, which sometimes settled on Tata like a thick black cloak, stifling him, they were happy. I knew that. Mama once said to me that loving somebody, *really* loving them and sharing things and being happy, is worth all the material goods in the world. I agreed out loud, but found myself thinking that it would be much better to be happy and loving in a fine house with lots of wonderful clothes and food. I didn't say that, of course. Perhaps because I couldn't have borne it if she had agreed with me. You want to feel your parents like their life, just in case it is your fault that they don't...

Anyway, suddenly, it seemed, they were not talking at all. Mama looked more weary and hopeless than ever, and Tata now seemed permanently sad and angry. Some nights he came home really late, and Mama would take his dinner out of the oven, all dried up, and put it down in front of him with a reproachful look.

"I met with Stefan," he said quietly.

"Again?"

"We have a lot to talk about," he said.

"I'm sure you have." Her voice was sarcastic. "Stefan is lucky."

"None of us are lucky, Rodika," he whispered, trying to reach for her hand.

She pulled it away. "You don't have to tell me that. You don't have to tell me what I know, Constantin," she said bitterly.

"Oh, but I do."

"There's no point in talking any more," she said, and rose to go into the kitchen, where the damp bubbled and sprouted on the walls and the wooden draining board was cracked down the middle.

Tata glanced at me, where I sprawled on their bed, pretending to do my homework. It was cold in the room, I thought, although the paraffin heater was lit, and the curtains drawn tightly against the world outside.

Suddenly the lights went out.

I froze.

In the kitchen, Mama burst into tears, whilst Tata crashed about, looking for the candlestick. He cursed the President, the economy, the lack of electricity – everything. At last light flickered from the table, mysterious and beautiful, and making his bearded face glow like an image of John the Baptist I saw once on an icon.

"What's the matter with Mama? Why is she upset?" I asked at last.

"Adults have quarrels – just like children," he replied. "By the way, have you made friends with Alys yet?"

"Oh yes – it was nothing," I said.

"That's my girl."

My mother was clattering plates in the sink. We both listened for a while, then my father raised his head and called out, "Rodika! Flora's friendly with Alys again!"

She stood at the kitchen door, her hands dripping, and said, "I knew that. She told me. I said it's silly to quarrel when …"

"… you don't know what tomorrow will bring," he finished.

"Exactly," she said.

There was a short silence, as my father and mother looked at each other and nodded, then looked at me, as if to show me how wise they were about my friendships. And then the lights went on as suddenly as they'd been extinguished.

I got up and went to my tiny bedroom, and lay on the bed, looking up at the cracks and stains on my ceiling. I could always see faces in them, or sometimes maps of other countries. Now I just saw a spider's web, in which I felt caught. How dare they act in that way? Pretending to be interested in me, when it was obvious that they were really talking about themselves? It seemed to me that in every single conversation there were three levels, and that all of us spoke different languages according to the level we were on at the time – like a lift going up and down.

First, there was the public language: what we all spoke in school, and on the stairs, and in the street. That was open, but at the same time utterly closed: you never ever said what you meant. Second, there was the private language, which you shared with your family and closest friends. The trouble with this was, it could work on so many levels of noncommunication too; just as in that little scene in the other room. And third, was your private, inner language: the words you spoke in your thoughts just to

24

yourself, the secrets you whispered wordlessly to the foggy mirror, and the wishes you would yell out on the wind, wildly, freely … but only on the solitary chocolate island of your dreams.

As I went to sleep at last, the radio was on in the next room, playing sad violin music. But I could still hear them talking in low, urgent voices, and it seemed that he was trying to persuade her of something, his voice putting out little hooks to grasp at her understanding, her … *permission*.

But for what?

I couldn't hear.

The next morning, in the blackness, I heard the front door slam. I knew it was Mama going out on her usual quest for bread, but instead of going back to sleep I sat up, and swung out of bed, gasping when my feet hit the icy linoleum. It took me just a few moments to dress, bundling myself into layer on layer of clothes, not caring how bulky and ugly I looked.

Tata was pulling up their bed. He looked round at me in surprise. "You're early."

There was a tiny noise at the door, more like an animal scratching than a knock. He jumped, and walked across putting his ear to the wooden panel. Someone whispered something, like a sigh in the blackness. My father nodded, satisfied, and opened the door.

An enormous man, wearing a stiff leather jacket and shapeless black trousers, filled the room. He and Tata nodded at each other.

"Mircea."

"Constantin."

"I saw Stefan last night," said my father.

"Good."

Then the man Mircea glanced at me.

"This is Flora," said my father anxiously, and I knew he wanted me gone.

"Hello, Flora," said the man.

I said nothing.

"Flora…"

I shrugged. "I expect you want me to go back to bed," I said coldly. "I have that feeling that you don't want me in here."

"I'll come back later," said the man.

"No, Mircea. Rodika…" my father began.

Then I felt really angry. It was obvious he had invited this man at a time he knew Mama would be out. Furiously I strode from the room, slamming the door of my room behind me. I lay on my bed in my clothes, hearing them whisper, trying to overhear.

But after only about eight minutes Mircea had obviously said what he had come to say, and I heard the door click shut behind him. When Mama came home at last bearing a loaf that was at least a day old, neither Tata nor I made any reference to the visitor. We chewed the bread miserably, then all went our separate ways. So that was another brick in the wall of silence that was being built between us all.

In school Daniel Ghiban quickly became very popular with most of the kids. He was generous — he gave his favoured ones bits of his packed meal most days, and it was always superior to everyone else's. He was strong and tough, and once, when he was jeered at (I can't remember why) by Ion Babeti who'd always ruled the roost, Daniel pretended to walk away, then turned before you could blink, got Ion in an armlock, and made him apologize. He never had any trouble after that, and to tell the truth, most of us thought him wonderful. He was a leader.

But here's where I come to the part that makes me feel strange. Daniel seemed to pick me out of the crowd. He gave me bites of his sandwiches (chicken … ham … salami … cheese… Oh, you can't imagine!). He would just hang around with me during those small pockets (not enough) of free school time. It was as if he had noticed me and helped me on his very first day, and that was a bond between us.

He had a fund of silly jokes too, which made me laugh more than I had laughed in years. Like, "A woman went into a shop, to ask for some meat. The man behind the counter shook his head in pity and led her to the door. 'No, Madam,' he said, 'over there is the butcher's. That's where they don't have meat. This is where we don't have cheese.'"

"You've never told us, Ghiban, how come you always have such decent food," Alys called out, when we were all standing round in a crowd, stamping our feet with the cold.

"It's a long story," he said with a grin.

"Tell us, we've got time," she said, in a challenging voice I knew very well. Our friendship was not what it was. We still walked to school together, but sometimes in the afternoon Alys went off a different way, and she was moody and quiet a lot of the time, as if she had something on her mind. But I didn't ask what.

"I'm not supposed to tell," he said. Yet he looked relaxed, as if nothing would ever worry him, standing there squarely, in his good jeans, and the padded bomber jacket that was the envy of the school.

"Don't you trust me, Ghiban?" asked Alys, with a mocking note in her voice I found unpleasant.

"It's not wise to trust anyone, Grosu," he replied calmly.

"That's what my mother says," I chipped in.

"I suppose you don't trust your friends if you've got something to hide," said Alys.

There was a silence. Everybody was looking at Daniel, waiting for him to speak. We didn't ever ask each other outright questions; it just wasn't done. When you are brought up right from the beginning to believe that your neighbour might be your worst enemy, you hold back. My mother even told me that in a queue the women don't complain to each other about the bread being stale, or the oil ration running out – for fear they will be overheard and reported. So this public challenge by Alys was daring – and frightening – somehow.

Daniel Ghiban shrugged, and lowered his voice. "Well, if you must know, it's my mother. She works as a cleaning lady for somebody in the British Embassy – somebody very important – and he pays her very well. He has to. He can't get good help otherwise. And his wife – she likes my mother and gives her things."

"Food?" I said, enviously.

He nodded. "They get stuff from England, you see. Every week they have supplies flown in. And the people at the Embassy give second-hand clothes away, so…" He shrugged and stopped. Then he lowered his head and added, "You probably think it's humiliating to take charity from foreigners, but my mother wants the best for me."

I was torn in two when he said that. A part of me admired his honesty, and felt touched by the fact that he seemed almost ashamed of what he had admitted. Open and free with each other – why couldn't we be more like that? I suspected that's how kids our age are in America or Britain, not scurrying round with your head down, as we do. And Alys seemed mean to me – a person who wanted to get her own back by showing up someone in public. But.

There was a serious But as well. Why should Daniel say all that stuff about humiliation? We were all green with envy; we'd all give anything for a few free presents. Why, we'd all seen our parents running desperately to be at the front of a queue, waiting patiently in Easter snow to buy us awful bits of stale chocolate from God knows where, even bribing the local Party officials with whatever they could, to get access to special deliveries at Christmas. Humiliation? That was part of being a Romanian. It went with the blood. It was in the soil. So what on earth was Daniel Ghiban talking about? It didn't ring true.

"OK, so what does your father do?" asked Alys.

"He's a hospital porter," Daniel replied shortly.

Then the buzzer went, and it was over.

Later, Alys and I were walking out of school

together when we heard running footsteps behind us. I clutched her arm, afraid to look round. But it was only Daniel Ghiban.

"Can I walk with you?" he asked pleasantly.

"I didn't know you lived this way," said Alys.

"*Alys!*" I protested.

It was a cold, golden autumn afternoon, the very end of October, when most of the trees have already shed their leaves and the city seems to breathe out the smell of a million paraffin stoves and as many lamps, smoky and pungent. And the people on the streets start to look mysterious – all muffled up, with hats pulled down over their eyes, and taking on that bundled, huddled, shapeless look of Winter strangers, so that you would hardly recognize your own mother, unless she spoke. I always dreaded winter. Walking from outside into our block was like drifting from ice into snow – only the cold inside was worse because it was damp and dank and clung to you.

Mama said she always regretted her bad timing, so that I was born at the beginning of November – because when I was a baby she and Tata used to make a sort of tent of bedclothes, to change my nappy underneath by the dangerous light of a candle, because that was the only way to keep me warm. She'd be washing nappies in icy water, so that her skin cracked, she told me.

Sometimes I hate the thought of growing up, if it has to be like that. The hardship. No escape.

I don't know why I started to think these gloomy thoughts – because the afternoon was beautiful, and Daniel Ghiban was smiling. Perhaps it was because I was with the two of them, I felt embarrassed that Alys had to be so unfriendly.

"We used to race sometimes," I said, "but she always beat me. I'm so small."

"Nothing wrong with being small," he grinned, "Chewing gum's not very big, but everybody wants it!"

"Yes, and cabbages are big, and they're boring!" I said, feeling pleased.

"Thanks," Alys said, looking down at me.

"Don't be silly," I said.

"Well, if you think I'm silly and boring, I'd better get out of your sight," she said, and started to run down the road, her hair bouncing up and down.

"Alys!" I called.

"Leave her," said Daniel.

"You're right," I said. He looked very sympathetic. "Alys can be so funny sometimes. We used to be so close, but now I've started to hate her moods. I don't understand it."

"Maybe..." he said, then stopped.

"What?"

"Nothing."

"Please tell me. We've been best friends for so long, and she's not the same. I…"

"Well, maybe she's … worried about something. Maybe she's got a guilty conscience," he said.

"What do you mean?" I asked, desperate for some explanation of Alys's moodiness.

"Oh nothing… I mean, I don't know."

We walked in silence, then suddenly he stopped. "I have to go now," he said.

"I wish you'd explain. About Alys," I said.

He shook his head. "I shouldn't have said anything. You'll only think I'm getting at her because she's been so down on me. Do you agree? She hasn't been exactly pleasant. Not like the rest of you."

"Oh, you're right," I agreed. "She's been pretty mean."

"So promise you won't think me unfair?"

"OK."

"Well, all I'll say is … don't tell her things."

"What things?"

"Anything… Oh, let's leave it. It's just that I've been watching you and, shall I tell you something? I think you're one of the nicest people I've ever met, Flora. But you're too open. Your face gives everything away."

I hung my head, feeling the blush spread, and glad that my black scarf was so thick. There was a sort of dazzle of light inside me, making me warm and happy, and blinding me – like the sun. I basked. I felt all my limbs relax. And of course, I didn't know what to say.

"Let's leave it, shall we?" His voice was gentle.

I nodded mutely, looked up and smiled – and then he had turned and gone, calling "See you tomorrow!" over his shoulder.

The next morning, when I came out of the block into the murky gloom, Alys wasn't there. I waited for a while, then realized she must have gone on ahead. For a second I felt stunned – as if someone had brutally removed a piece from the puzzle that was my life, so that nothing hung together any more. There was a black hole.

But then the hole was filled with sadness. I thought of Alys and I pushing our funny old dolls around in our little home-made carts when we were tiny, and playing make-believe games, and sitting on the steps in the summer as we got older, and talking. We'd had such good times; it had always been me and Alys against the world. I knew that things changed as you grew up. At school people were always making and breaking friendships, but I never thought it would happen to us.

Alys had changed. It wasn't me, it was her.

Then I felt cross. I thought of how unfair it was, and how mean she could be, and how kind and sympathetic Daniel Ghiban had been when he told me… what? Not to trust Alys? But *Alys?* Yet she had changed; she wasn't the friend I'd known all my life; so anything was possible.

She didn't speak to me at school.

I hung around with Mariana and Luminitsa, two girls I quite liked, and who were always talking to Daniel. At lunchtime he came up to us, put his hand in his pocket and pulled out … *A STICK OF WRIGLEY'S CHEWING GUM!*

"Here," he said. "Share this."

But it was me he handed it to.

Feeling very proud, I tore it roughly into three, and we clutched each other in ecstasy, holding the bits on our tongues; not even sucking, let alone chewing, so that the minty taste would slowly, very slowly flood our mouths. Then you suck it a bit. Then – you can't stop the urge – you let your teeth bite into the thin stuff, and feel it change and stretch, and, oh … *amazing*! I think that must have been only the third time in my whole life I'd tasted it. It was almost a myth: like Christmas.

So I forgot about Alys. I knew that if I'd been standing with her I wouldn't have had the treat. Three days later, on Saturday, it was my birthday. Mama let me sleep late, and it was ten before I woke. She was sitting on my bed, tickling my cheek. I blinked.

"Happy Birthday, darling!" she whispered.

"I'm thirteen!" I said sleepily, just beginning to realize.

"Really grown up!" Mama said tenderly.

"Do I look different?" I asked, sitting up quickly.

She laughed. "Oh yes, your hair is sticking up more than ever, and you've lost some weight in the night because you're hungry! So get dressed and come through. There's a special present for breakfast!"

I pulled on my shirt, trousers and sweater, and rushed through to the main room. Tata was sitting in a chair, smiling at me. Mama had set the table for one, with some orange gladioli in a vase — just three splendid spikes.

"It looks lovely," I said.

She told me to sit down. There was one card and one little brown parcel at my place.

"Not yet!" said Tata, as I reached out.

I quickly changed the direction of my hand, and squeezed the bread.

"It's fresh!" I cried.

"A special day," said Tata, "The man in the bakery knew."

"Did he?" I asked, and he laughed.

Then Mama walked in from the kitchen and put down a plate in front of me. I stared. There were two pieces of salami and a little strip of cheese.

"Oh!" I cried, and went to pick up my knife and fork.

"Not yet!" said Tata again.

Mama had disappeared back into the kitchen, and came back with the frying pan. With a huge smile, and a theatrical flourish, she ladled a fried egg on to my plate. A FRIED EGG!

"Happy Birthday, little Flora!" she said.

"Not so little now!" said my father.

I took a slice of bread and dipped it into the egg, and imagined that heaven must be like this. You'd have an egg for breakfast every day, and all would be right with the world. After the first taste I cut everything up into little strips so it would last a long time, and it didn't matter that the egg went cold, and some of the bits round the edge were tough and burnt. It was my birthday treat and I didn't want it to disappear quickly into the black cavern of my stomach, so that I'd never see it again. I wanted it to *stay with me*. Like everything really.

"Now you can open," said Mama, when I'd finished.

I opened the envelope first. It was a card showing a bunch of lovely flowers in pale pinks and blues, with a gold line all round the edge. And it said *Bon Anniversaire* in French – which I thought terribly smart. She had written, "A Happy Birthday to our big girl, and deepest love from your loving parents." When I looked up to say thank you, the room seemed to swim a little bit before my eyes.

Then I took the parcel. It was soft. Although it was only wrapped in the same brown paper we used for sandwiches and everything, Mama had taken my old paints and drawn little moons and stars all over, so it looked really pretty. I unfolded the tucks at the end very carefully, so that I wouldn't spoil it. My heart was thudding. I could still smell the egg. My hands shook as I finally spread the paper out to reveal what was inside.

It was a scarf. Not a woolly muffler, like we all wear to school to keep the cold out. No, this was a really smart scarf, a ladies' scarf – the sort of thing you wear to look nice. It was silky, and quite big, and patterned with vague patterns of flowers, abstract really, in scarlet, green and black. It was the first grown-up present I had ever had: something unnecessary and ... glamorous.

I rushed into the bathroom, folded it into a triangle, and put it around my neck, knotting it in front. Then I looked in the old foggy mirror. My hair was dark, my face was pale, my sweater was black, and the new scarf made everything glow. I pulled it to one side, so that the knot was almost on my shoulder and I thought that I looked like an actress.

Grown up at last.

Almost … beautiful.

I didn't run back into the room, I walked like a lady. But when I saw Mama's face, anxious that I should like the present, I couldn't keep up the pose, and rushed to hug her.

"It's lovely. Thank you," I whispered.

"Thank Tata too."

It was always Mama who made things happen, and got presents – and anyway I was still a bit cross with my father because of the morning the man Mircea came round – but he was smiling happily, and so I kissed him too.

"*He chose it, Flora*," said Mama, "What good taste!"

"Thank you, Tata. It's the nicest present I've ever had," I said.

"Such a grown-up girl…" he started to say, then suddenly pulled me to him and clutched me as if he would never let me go. I couldn't breathe. His chest heaved, as if he was trying to control his emotions. When at last I pulled back, I saw his eyes were wet. "What's the matter, Tata?" I asked.

"Nothing, darling, he's just proud of you," said Mama quietly, fiddling with the scarf to rearrange it.

"People change so quickly. Grow so quickly," said Tata, in a strange intense voice that seemed to come from far away.

But I wasn't listening. I went back to the bathroom, took the scarf off, and came back with it knotted round my head, like a gypsy. It made them laugh. Then Mama tried it on and I said she could borrow it, and we all took the tram to the city centre to walk up and look at the President's dreadful, lavish, new, giant palace, with all the cranes still around it, and the long avenues with empty fountains. My father whispered that the whole Romanian people could fit inside it, and be safe from the fascists. Mama said "Shhh", of course, but she smiled. We bought hot chestnuts from a man in the street, and went wandering up the Calei Victoria, looking at the ruby glass in the more expensive shops. They told me stories about when they were young, and when I was a baby, and we laughed a lot. All together. All talking.

It was a happy day, that last day of my childhood. It was after that, as winter came, that the bad things began to happen.

THREE

It was a normal, quiet Sunday, the day after my birthday.

I was doing my homework, Mama was mending her tights, my father was on his hands and knees replacing the wick of the paraffin stove. As a result, we were rather cold. I even had my black muffler on. The silky red scarf was laid carefully in the top drawer in my bedroom, for special occasions. Mama had made a potato and onion soup for lunch, and already the savoury smell filled the room, making me hungry.

Suddenly there was a knock. My father looked up sharply, my mother stared anxiously at him, and I glanced at the clock on the wall, wondering who would come at this time on a Sunday morning. Then I felt a huge leap of excitement. It would be Alys – I was sure of that. Alys knew it was my birthday. She must be feeling sorry that we had quarrelled and had decided to come over to make friends.

I jumped up. "I expect it's Alys," I said, and then my parents relaxed once more, like puppets when the puppet-master slackens the strings.

As I explained, our apartment consists of just one room, for living, eating and my parents' sleeping (the sofa bed is really very comfortable), with a small galley kitchen off it. You go out into the small hall, and there's the door to my bedroom, the door to the bathroom, and the front door. When I went out to the front door, I closed the living room door behind me, thinking that Alys and I might feel shy and awkward, so it would be better for us to be private.

There was another knock, slight and hesitant, as if the person was worried that this might be the wrong place. It was odd. It wasn't how Alys usually knocked. Suddenly I felt nervous, and I was just about to go back into the living room to fetch my father when I remembered I was thirteen now, and ought not to behave like a baby.

So I opened the door. It was gloomy on the landing, as usual, so for a moment I couldn't see who was there – just a shadowy outline. Then the person stepped forward – and I wanted to die with confusion and delight.

It was Daniel Ghiban.

He shifted from one foot to the other, and then held out his hand, balled into a fist. He muttered, "Look Flora, I heard ... I heard it was your birthday yesterday. And so I want you to have these. As a present."

Turning over his hand, he uncurled his fingers – and there, on his palm, was a packet of sweets. Chocolate sweets from the West that I had heard about, but never seen. They were quite famous, actually, like Levi's and Coca-Cola and Kent cigarettes, but to me much more desirable than all those put together. A real packet of M&Ms. All bright and real and miraculous; lying there on his outstretched palm, and being offered to ME.

"Go on," he said.

I couldn't speak. I looked at him, then the sweets, then back at him, and I knew I looked like a fish, with my mouth gaping stupidly. At last I stuttered, "I didn't... It's ... I mean, I ... oh, thank you." Then reached out reverently and took the little packet.

Just then the living room door opened, and my father was there. "Who...?" he began, then stopped. He looked at Daniel and a shutter came down over his face. It was the usual response to a stranger – or at least, an adult stranger.

"Tata — this is a boy from my class, Daniel Ghiban, the new boy. He brought me a present. Look! For my birthday — chocolate sweets!" I held them out on my palm, and couldn't stop the grin from spreading all over my face.

"Oh," he said, looking suspiciously from the M&Ms to Daniel, then back to the sweets.

"I'll go now," said Daniel.

"You don't have to," I said, embarrassed because my father was being so unfriendly.

"I've got homework to do," said Daniel.

"I'll walk down to the bottom of the stairs with you — just to say thank you," I said, trying to sound sophisticated and carefree.

"You've got school work as well, Flora. Be sensible," said my father shortly.

"But look, Tata!" I said, pleading with my eyes, holding out the packet of chocolates.

"Very nice. A very kind thought," he said, in a gruff formal voice.

"OK — I'll see you tomorrow," said Daniel, in his usual easygoing voice, as if he'd known us for ever, and my father had just treated him like a favourite nephew, instead of an enemy of the people.

"Goodbye — and thank you!" I called, as he disappeared back down the murky stairwell.

My father was standing looking out of the window, with his back to the room. There was nothing to see out there, just the towering blocks with their rows and rows of dark windows, like little eyes, all watching. Cigarette smoke drifted about his head, like a cloud – warning me there'd be trouble.

But I ignored him.

"Look, Mama," I said, holding out my hand.

She gasped when she saw the sweets. "But you can only get those from the dollar shops, or on the black market!" she said.

"No – Daniel's mother works for an important man in the British Embassy," I said, feeling I had to defend this amazing gift, and resenting the fact at the same time. "They give her things. She's really lucky."

"She certainly is," said Mama, wistfully.

Then my father turned round abruptly. "It's not right," he said.

"What?" I asked.

"I don't want boys coming to this place to see you. You're too young," he said.

"Tata, I'm thirteen years old, for one thing. And for another thing, Daniel Ghiban is just a nice, kind boy who wants to be my friend, which makes a change in this world!"

"He's a stranger," said my father.

"No, he's not. He's in my class."

"You don't know him. You don't know where he came from. You have to be careful."

I lost my temper then, and flung Daniel's present down on the table. "Careful, careful! I suppose you think he's put poison in these or something. Is that what you think?"

"Huh – presents… It's not normal," he said.

"What do you *mean*?" I cried out in frustration.

"People don't do things like that. People look after themselves. He must want something."

"Constantin – the child's delighted. Don't spoil it for her … and such a wonderful surprise," murmured Mama gently.

"You're the one who's always warning *me* to be careful," he said, giving her a look I couldn't understand.

"Children, Constantin! They're *children*," she said.

"Oh God," he said, crossing the room in a couple of strides, and slumping into his chair.

I looked from one to the other and felt, as always, that there was a different story written in invisible ink between the lines of their speech.

"Come here, Flora," he said at last, in a quiet, almost apologetic voice.

Reluctantly I went and stood by him, and when he reached and took my hand I left it limp, because I didn't want to respond.

"People have to look after themselves," he said. I was silent. "You see," he went on wearily, "there are so many things I can't explain to you, but you have to understand that I'm right when I say it isn't wise to be friendly to strangers. You just have to believe me."

"But then you'd make no new friends," I protested.

"People like us can't afford the luxury of new friends, Flora."

"I don't believe that. It's like locking yourself in a prison," I said angrily, pulling my hand away.

He laughed then. "A prison! My dear child, we live in a prison. Only it's a really big one, with guards all round its border, and it's our whole beloved country. The trouble is, most people get used to it. They like their prison, because they're terrified of trying to leave it. So they all shuffle round in the huge prison yard, heads down, doing what the guards tell them. For ever." His laugh was harsh.

"Oh, Constantin," said Mama wearily, and went into the kitchen. For a second the only sound was the stirring of her soup.

"You make it sound like my fault!" I said.

He looked up quickly, as if I had hit on a truth. But I picked up my M&Ms, and went into my bedroom without saying another word, closing the door behind me. For a long time I sat looking at the packet, not wanting to open it, just enjoying the possession.

Finally I tore a hole across one corner, tipped out five or six into my palm, inspected them carefully, then chose a red one. I put it on my pillow, and posted the others back through the little hole. My heart was beating fast now. I put out my tongue, and placed the red sweet in the middle, relishing the sensation – all round and smooth – as I closed my mouth around it. But I didn't bite, not yet. The few moments of not-biting were wonderfully tantalizing: the delicious moment postponed, until I could resist it no more, and my teeth cracked the sugar shell, releasing the first burst of chocolate on my tongue.

As I lay back, letting it melt and flood my mouth, I remembered the fantasy island of my childhood dreams, and thought with amusement that if I had known then about M&Ms, it would have been far more colourful – a tropical beach strewn with reds, greens and yellows. But I wouldn't want to be on it alone any more. That was the kind of solitary selfishness my father was preaching, and I rebelled against it. In my daydream, as my tongue chased the last traces of chocolate around my mouth, I thought what fun it would be to have a friend on the island, someone like Daniel. And we would have two small huts to live in (at opposite ends, I thought, because you'd want some privacy and peace), and not have any grown-ups telling us what to do. Not my father, nor the old Monster at school, nor horrible Ceauşescu who made everybody miserable, and yet lived a life of luxury in the palace he built in the ruins of Bucharest. Awful, appalling adults...

There, I thought, even the nicest daydreams are spoilt. You can't keep them out. They invade your mind. I hate them all.

The pleasure had gone. I sat up, looked at the sweets and resisted the temptation to cram them all in my mouth at once. Instead, I opened the top drawer and laid them very carefully on top of my silky red, black and green scarf. Then I didn't close the drawer, but stood looking at the display with some pride, but some sadness too.

First, of course, I felt that I was the luckiest person in the city. We didn't have many things, I knew that, and so these two presents in the drawer represented so much to me. Somewhere in the world, I realized, (because I had read, and we talked endlessly of such things) ladies wore scarves made of real silk, not rayon, and people ate chocolates all day if they wanted too. And chewing gum. And fruity sweets in wrappers with twists at the end. But that was *there*. I was *here*.

And so I felt thrilled to own the scarf, and decided that I'd allow myself to eat two or three sweets only, each night, to make them last, I wouldn't share them with anyone, not even Mama and Tata! Then I would keep the empty packet for ever. Each time I took a peep my lovely things would shine out at me, like hidden gold.

I thought, I *want*, I *want*, I *want*, I *want*...

But secondly, there was a part of me that felt ashamed that I should attach so much importance to such things – only objects after all. I remembered a day when Mama had come home looking even more triumphant than usual, and when she unpacked her shopping bag we saw why.

"Toilet paper – look!" she said, her eyes bright with excitement. We all shared it with her, and Tata carried the roll off to the bathroom, held high in his hands as if it were a ceremonial flag or something. But a few minutes later, Mama sat down at the table heavily, and buried her face in her hands.

"What is it, Mama?" I asked, frightened that she felt ill.

"Oh, nothing," she said, raising her head. "It's just that ... oh, Constantin, I suddenly thought that my day has been made because I managed to find some toilet paper. *Toilet paper!* You know – you could be excited because you've got a book you've always wanted, or something pretty for the apartment, or a really good present for Flora, or some tickets for a play… But no. You feel joy at toilet paper. So *base*. That's what they have done to our souls."

I remember he nodded, then put his arms round her without saying a word, so that I felt excluded, and didn't know why.

Now I pictured their hug, then recalled their recent rows and thought that all the possessions in the world weren't as important as love. And friendship… Then I wondered if Alys had thought of me that weekend. In the old days I'd have rushed to show her my scarf and my sweets but not now. Something had gone, and my glorious presents went only part way to consoling me.

So I looked at the two things in the drawer and couldn't help seeing them as opposites, standing for two halves of life. The scarf (I reached out and touched it with my finger, so silky-smooth) represented my mother and father, and our whole life together up to that point, when suddenly I had grown up and became aware of things I hadn't seen before. I hated that – the fact that I suddenly saw my father as mean and bad-tempered and secretive and unfriendly, and that a part of me could even criticize Mama for retreating to the kitchen whenever there was a bad atmosphere, instead of standing up to him.

The M&Ms represented a dream, and luxury, and privilege, of course ... but also something new I knew nobody understood: a longing within me to be liked – sort of, as a grown-up. The fact was that Daniel Ghiban, the handsome and popular one, was the first boy to have treated me like a person. And this knowledge awoke little longings inside me I hadn't known were there – to be independent, to be good-looking, to be admired. Just like Daniel.

One half of me, with the memory of chocolate still in her mouth, felt excited and rebellious. The other half, which remembered the simple taste of roast chestnuts in the street, and the feeling of my arms tucked in my parents', felt guilty and uncertain and afraid.

From the room next door I heard my parents' voices raised in anger once again.

Then I smelt it.

The terrible, acrid smell of burnt soup.

And I wanted to cry, because I sensed it was all my fault, but I didn't really know why. So I slammed the drawer shut, and stood in the cold room alone, suddenly wishing with all my heart that Daniel Ghiban had not come.

FOUR

It was not long afterwards that the world turned upside down – at least as far as my father was concerned. If I tell you it made little difference to me, that I didn't even know about it until a couple of days later, you'll probably think me dim or something. But it was like that for a lot of people much older than me. The point is, when you're in a prison you can be thinking so hard about the key, focussing on that imaginary key in the great, thick iron door, that you don't even notice that a little stone has fallen from the wall at the other end of your cell, letting in a chink of light.

So.

On 9 November 1989, the wall between East and West Berlin was opened. Then my father, Constantin Popescu, aged 36, small, dark and excitable was plunged first into a state of delirious happiness, and then (just as quickly) into a deeper despair than I had ever seen.

Even at school we had heard rumours of change "out there" – in Hungary, Poland, Czechoslovakia – like the awful, ugly old buildings were shaking at their foundations, and falling down. I knew we all lived in a system called Communism, or Socialism. In school we were taught how bad life was in the West under the opposite system, Capitalism. We knew for a fact, because they told us, that the rich people lived off the poor people, that there were no jobs or homes, that people killed themselves in their misery. The vast invisible barrier that stretched round all our countries in the Eastern Block (which was made concrete in the actual Berlin Wall itself) was to keep OUT the destructive enemy forces of fascism. We weren't allowed to travel there because we would be corrupted. And so on. That was what our teachers said.

Of course, most of us probably got a different message at home – that the borders, with the guards and the dogs and the wire, were there to keep us IN. That's what my father said.

So now my father saw one wall being taken down – the wall the world saw as a symbol. But once he had got over his excitement and disbelief, he said it made him feel the wall around US was all the higher.

On Monday 13 November there was a strange new atmosphere at school – a sense of strain, and of waiting. Even before classes began, some of the older students stood around in small knots, whispering. Their faces were tense and excited. Quickly teachers moved amongst them and broke up the groups, but although the older teenagers were sullen they didn't seem as intimidated as usual.

Then two mysterious things happened. A boy in our class called Maryon was called to see the Principal. This was a surprise, because he was a quiet, weedy boy with big, sticky-out ears and funny glasses, and he never, ever got into trouble. He went white when he was told, walked slowly from the room with his head down, and didn't come back into class. At the end of the afternoon someone said they had seen him being driven away in a black car with two men. But people say all sorts of things. You never know if they are true. Rumours run up and down every school, factory and office like flame on a leak of paraffin. You never know what to believe.

But this we did know. Next morning our form teacher, known as the old Monster by everyone, was not at his desk. We all thought he must be ill, even though the idea was ridiculous. The Monster was, we all fervently believed, put on this earth with the holy task of making his pupils' lives a misery, and never, ever showed any weakness in carrying out this duty. So he couldn't possibly be ill. He'd live for ever, like Dracula.

One of the other teachers took the register, and put us through all our usual patriotic stuff. She was just going out when Alys piped up, "Will Mr Paroan be back soon, Miss?" The look she was given would have even turned back Dracula from a nice juicy neck.

"Paroan has left, Grosu. He won't be coming back," was the icy reply.

Then the teacher slammed the door behind her, as if she'd been given a personal insult. Something was wrong, it was obvious. Why should the Monster leave like that? We stopped calling him his nickname from that moment, as if we sensed he wasn't so bad after all.

"Have some," said Daniel, holding out his packet.

"What have you got today?" I asked.

"Only sausage," he said.

"Mmmm." My mouth was already full.

We stood together, slightly apart from the others. It was often like that now – although Daniel was as popular as ever. He seemed to make a point of talking to everyone, yet I had the feeling that he liked best to be with me. Sometimes he would slip me a whole piece of chewing gum – but only when he knew nobody was watching. Sometimes this made me guilty, and I longed to be able to go up to Alys, tear the stick in half, and share it with her. Of course, I never did. For one thing I knew she wouldn't accept such an obvious overture of friendship.

Anyway, I thought, *why should I share with anyone?*

At last I finished eating, and hesitated before saying what was on my mind. I suppose it was custom: you didn't ask people questions unless you'd known them for years and years. Then presumably you'd be able to read their mind anyway.

"Daniel... What do you think about this business with the Berlin Wall?" I asked finally.

"What do you think?" he countered.

"I don't know... My father..."

"What?"

"Nothing."

"Tell me, Flora," he said gently.

"Um – people are different, aren't they?" I said, not saying what I had been going to say.

"Your father?"

"No – people. There's a new feeling in the air."

"It won't last," he said decisively. "Not here.

You wait and see."

He sounded utterly convinced, and perfectly satisfied too. It was strange, but it reassured me.

"What do you think's wrong with the old M ... with Mr Paroan?" I asked, wanting to change the subject, in case he asked about my father again.

"I think maybe the Monster's being taught a lesson by somebody else, just for a change," he said, with an odd, harsh note in his voice.

"Who?"

"Who knows?" he shrugged. "I'll tell you something, though. Two people have gone, the Monster and Maryon. And I saw the same person deep in conversation with them both, at separate times, last week. And I saw this same person talking to a man in a car, after school. Looks suspicious to me."

"Who was it?" I gasped, ready, as we all were, to listen to any rumour that would answer all the questions. It was like a disease, this dependence on gossip, this readiness to seize on it and embroider what we'd heard.

"Your friend Alys," he said.

In the few seconds which followed that statement my mind travelled a couple of hundred miles in fast circles, so that I wanted to faint. I thought of the gulf between Alys and me.

"She isn't my friend any more," I said.

*   *   *

When I got home from school Tata was there already, which was unusual. He jumped guiltily, and pushed a book back into the crowded, rickety shelf unit, as if caught out doing something wrong.

"Why are you here so early?" I asked.

"We were sent home — production stopped because of the electricity," he said.

I hit the switch, but of course nothing happened. The room was full of the darkening grey of a November afternoon, damp and chill. Out of habit I went through to the kitchen and came back with two candleholders which I set up ready, although we wouldn't light them until absolutely necessary, because of the extravagance. I sighed. Doing my homework by candlelight was a strain. But maybe the lights would go back on soon.

"I'm going out, Flora," said Tata. "Your mother asked me to try to get some fruit, and I heard there might be some at the back of the supermarket. OK?"

I nodded. It didn't worry me to be left alone, even on such a dreary, dwindling day. Mama always used to tell me when I was little that only foolish children were afraid of ghosts and goblins and things that make noises in the night. "It's the real people you have to be afraid of," she would say.

As soon as the door closed behind my father I

rushed over to the shelf unit, to see what book he had been looking at. Was it fat, or thin? Blue, or red? I couldn't remember. So I pulled out a volume of folk tales and flicked through it – then thought. It had been on that shelf, I was sure. Next to the tales was the one book in the house you can be sure he wouldn't have looked at – a volume of Ceauşescu's speeches. We had it because ... well, you had to have such things. Just in case.

Something made me take out the fat book. On the jacket was a highly coloured photograph of our President, taken at least twenty years earlier, so that this eternally young, impossibly rosy-cheeked man beamed out at me. I opened the pages in the middle, and then nearly dropped the book in shock. Because someone had cut out the pages to make a secret compartment, and there, hidden in the centre of Ceauşescu's interminable speeches was ... money. I had never seen such money. There were green dollars in little rolls, and brightly coloured Deutschmarks. American and German banknotes ... hard currency, we called it, what everyone dreamt of, and what some men would kill their grandmothers to obtain. Our own money, the grubby lei, was worthless. To deal on the black market, to get American cigarettes, to bribe people, you needed hard currency. And here it was –

hidden in my own home. It looked like a fortune. But what was it doing there? How long had he been collecting it – and how? Did Mama know?

The evening seemed to pass very slowly. It should have been happy. The electricity went back on. Mama had managed to find a bit of chicken, which she made into a stew, with potato and onion and cabbage. It was the most delicious meal we had had in a long time, and yet I could barely taste it. I kept glancing at my father, and thinking of that mutilated book just across the room. It was as if a silent monster was crouched on the shelf, waiting to devour us all.

I couldn't wait to retreat to my room, although Mama asked me if I felt ill. She could tell something was wrong.

"I've got a sore throat," I lied, wanting to escape from them.

When my light was out I tried to sleep, but the vision of that currency kept dancing in front of my eyes in the darkness, mocking me with my lack of understanding. What was he saving for? It couldn't possibly be for Christmas.

I must have dozed off, because when I woke the room seemed much colder. I glanced across to the wall, and indeed the little flame of my own paraffin heater had been turned off, as usual. One of them must have crept in.

But they hadn't gone to bed. As usual, I could hear the radio, playing folk music. Behind it, they were talking, in those controlled intense tones they always used for a row. Yet this wasn't a row; their voices weren't angry. Even though I couldn't make out the words I could tell the discussion was serious, as if words were being weighed very carefully before being dropped into the pool. My mind full of that hidden money and all that had happened during the day, I knew I had to hear.

Careful not to make my bed creak, I got up. It took me a long time to lower the handle of my door, and inch it open, and creep out into the hall. My bare feet made no sound on the icy linoleum. I was in luck – the living room was open just a crack.

"You understand now, Rodi," he said.

"I ... well ... we've been through it so often it's a relief to have come to a decision," said Mama, with a big sigh. "I did think, when the news came from Germany, that you'd wait. I thought things might change here. You thought it too, at first..."

He broke in. "Rodika my darling! We've got to be realistic. You know we're different. The Czechs, the Poles – they've always had it easy, compared to us. This place will never change. That's why I got so depressed. All the good news just rubbed my nose in our own situation. When the old Cobbler dies there's two equally bad sons to take his place. So what hope is there?"

"None," she said. And her voice was so sad and low it made me want to cry.

"So – I've got no choice, Rodi. Please understand. I have to do it," he said, in a low, pleading voice.

"What if you…?" she began.

"I won't. It'll work, I promise you!"

"They shoot people," she cried.

"No," he said. "I'll make it."

"Then what? How long will it be?"

"Oh Rodi – how can I know. But you'll apply to join me, you and Flora, and in time they'll let you. They have to. It may be hard – but I believe this is the only chance for a better life for all of us."

I could see them through the door. They both got up, and enveloped each other in a massive hug before breaking apart and carrying on talking, still with their arms around each other.

"I can take it, Constantin – for your sake."

"For all our sakes," he said.

"But you're the one who's going," she said wistfully. "And if anything goes wrong, we'll be the ones left here."

"I know," he said.

"When…" her voice faltered again. "When will it happen?"

"Not for a while. The colder it is the better. Mircea and Stefan know the route, and they say the border guards there skive off on the coldest nights. Anyway, now I've got your backing I can carry on planning."

"Did you need my permission, my love?" asked Mama, in a sad, faraway voice, as if she had long given up the struggle.

"I need you to believe in me," said Tata.

And they clung to each other again, as if all the soldiers and secret police in the world would not be able to break them apart. I heard the muffled words, "I love you", but I couldn't see anything any more. Blindly I backed away, and I don't know how I got back to my bedroom without them hearing me. But then, they were too involved in their own drama to think about me.

Lying in my bed in the pitch darkness, I felt as if I was tossing in a tiny boat on some vast, black ocean. There was nothing around me any more, nothing to keep me safe, only the howling of the wind and the beating of the rain. And the rain was the tears which poured down my cheeks, whilst my secret, silent voice howled out a long cry of pain. At last I knew what it all meant.

He was getting the currency from somewhere, and making plans with his friends to cross the border. He would go, and Mama and I would be left behind. Maybe we would never see him again, but that was a price he was obviously prepared to pay – and she was letting him.

My father was going to leave us.

FIVE

In the weeks that followed it was as if I was living on an island, only it wasn't the island of my dreams. This one was cold and lonely, and certainly not made of chocolate. It wasn't a fantasy. My misery and rage were real – and I couldn't tell anyone.

When you find something out it changes your whole life – only backwards as well as forwards. So I thought of my birthday and felt angry because all the time my parents were deceiving me. I wondered for how long. So everything was spoilt.

I don't know if my parents noticed I was different. One day Mama said, "You've been very quiet lately, Flora. Is something wrong at school?"

When I shook my head she didn't ask any more questions. *What do you care?* I thought, *You're too worried about him to care about me.* If she had only told me herself, treated me like a friend, I could have borne the whole thing much better. But maybe parents find it hard to think of their children as friends.

And when my father tried to put an arm round me one day, and make a little joke about thirteen-year-olds getting moody overnight, as bad as grown-up women, I pulled away. He shrugged, but I could see he was hurt. I didn't care. It was fair that he should suffer. Fair. After all, Mama was a victim like me — but he was the one who was getting out. All I could think of was that he was prepared to leave behind the people he loved to get his own freedom. Strangely, I never imagined him being caught on the border and beaten up then thrown in prison, or even being shot. My imagination couldn't stretch to that horror. No, the truth is, I imagined him having a great time in Germany, France or England, or (best of all) the United States of America. Eating wonderful food. Listening to Phil Collins and the Beatles and Madonna. Wearing Levis ... all that.

I know I was stupid. And ignorant. I thought refugees from Romania would be welcomed with open arms wherever they wanted to go, and ... sort of ... given all these goodies. As if! But we all believed that some sort of heaven existed beyond the borders of our poor little country. There were places where people could actually vote for their leaders and read free newspapers and watch other things on television than Ceauşescu jawing, jawing, jawing.

The word *Freedom* doesn't mean much to you when you're young and you've never had it. It's a great *idea*, but you can't taste, touch or smell an idea. So translate it into the freedom to eat chocolate and sweets ... and it starts to have meaning. I think I saw the West as some huge shop where everything was free.

And my father was choosing that. It meant more to him than we did. If it didn't, then he wouldn't be going.

Isn't that what *you* would think?

School was worse than ever, mainly because we found out at last what all of us had suspected. The word went round quickly. Our form teacher, Mr Paroan, the Old Monster, had been arrested. They said he had been seen talking to a foreign spy. Or maybe he was a spy himself. It was impossible to know the truth because everybody guessed this or that. We talked about it in whispers.

"I can't imagine the Old – him – doing anything wrong. He was always so down on us."

"Serve him right then."

"That's not fair."

"He was never very fair."

"No worse than the others."

"Better than some."

"He wasn't really a bad bloke."

"You didn't say that when he swiped your head with his ruler!"

And so on – round and round.

We had a new form teacher, called Miss Creanu. She was terrible: tall and thin with a face like an animal trap. Once she heard us talking about Maryon, and punished us all by keeping us in during the break to work out maths problems. She made Mr Paroan seem like St Nicholas. Already I found myself remembering only the nice things about him, despite what one or two people in the class said.

Maryon. That story was much nearer home, somehow, because Maryon was one of us. Or, at least, he had been. His story was easier to find out, although you still had to depend on rumours, which may or may not have been true. They said he had been telling bad jokes about Comrade Ceauşescu in school, and that his father held secret meetings in their apartment, and was an enemy of the country.

"How do they know that?" I asked Mariana.

"Somebody told," she whispered.

"Who would do a thing like that?"

"There's always somebody," she said, looking over her shoulder.

They said Maryon had been called to see the Principal, and given a good grilling by him. That would be enough to finish anybody off, in my opinion. In the end he did break down, and somebody took him home, and then they arrested his dad. And Maryon didn't ever come back to school. Nobody knew where he and his mother and little sister went.

"Probably to stay with relatives," said Daniel. "Anyway, it's none of our business."

"Best to keep your nose clean," agreed Mariana.

We were standing in a little group. Alys was on the edge, but suddenly strode forward, her face scarlet. "Oh yes, close your eyes so you don't see what's going on. Stop up your ears so you don't hear bad jokes about the President. Keep your mouth shut so you never tell the truth," her voice was terrifyingly loud.

"Shhh," I said.

Everybody looked shocked at her outburst, and I was afraid one of the teachers might have heard. But she didn't care. She gave me such a look of pity I wanted the ground to open up and bury me.

"Oh, shhhh," she mimicked, "because that's much easier, isn't it, Flora?"

"Well, it's certainly much safer," said Daniel Ghiban calmly, as if coming to my defence.

"You should know, Ghiban," said Alys, glaring at him.

"What do you mean, Grosu?" he asked, in that same, level grown-up voice, which made her sound hysterical and silly.

"I mean, you're pretty safe, with all your foreign goodies, and no questions asked!"

He raised his eyes to heaven. Most people would have lost their temper at that, and I admired him for being so relaxed and calm. He gave the slightest of shrugs and started to walk away. Over his shoulder he said loudly, "Talking about questions, Alys Grosu, I saw you spending lots of time with Maryon just before he got into trouble. I think you probably knew more about him than anyone."

Daniel strolled off, hands in his pockets. Alys's high colour disappeared with shocking speed, leaving her looking white and ill. I thought she was going to cry, or say something else; instead she just turned and ran off. The rest of us looked at each other in silence, then we all drifted away.

From that moment it was as if Alys was set apart. Usually, in gymnastics, pupils stood around admiringly to watch her cartwheels and back bends and flips. She was so much better than everyone else. They said she would be selected for the national squad. I used to be proud of her (although jealous too), when we were best friends...

But now people didn't pay her attention in the old way. And Alys didn't show off like she used to – as if she wanted to be private.

As if she had something to hide.

There was a nasty atmosphere of mistrust in our class – and I think, in the whole school. In a way we were used to that – brought up to be careful and secretive. But this was worse than ever. I felt as if everybody was waiting for something to happen – something to break the tension.

In lessons, I noticed, we were getting more propaganda than ever about our country. The President and his doings seemed to come into every single lesson. When it was geography we were told what an amazing world leader he was, and how, when he visited England, he had met the Queen – so highly did they think of him. In history we learnt about how he had taken Romania from its bad times into a future of glittering prosperity. In grammar we were read bits of his speeches, and told how they represented the best examples of our written language. In science we were told how the President's wife, Elena, was a brilliant scientist whom all of us must try to follow, for the good of our country. And so on, and so on.

No wonder we all longed for sport!

In the old days I would have told all this to my mother and father, to see what they thought. But I couldn't tell them anything now, and it made me feel lonelier than ever.

At least there were no more arguments at night when I had gone to bed. Mama and Tata had come to an agreement, and now they behaved more like young lovers than a married couple. If I hadn't overheard the Plan, I would have been delighted. He came home one night with a little parcel, which he presented to her with a flourish. It was a bar of good soap. She squealed with delight, and sniffed it so hard, you'd have thought she was going to eat it. He didn't say where he got it, of course, and she didn't ask. So much went unspoken.

They would sit quietly on the couch, holding hands, and he would do something I had never seen – go up behind her in the kitchen when she was preparing food, and put his arms around her waist and bury his face in her long dark hair. He helped more too, putting the knives and forks out, and washing the dirty dishes. It was all lovely.

But because I knew the real reason behind his affection it made me more angry and unhappy than ever. He was loving her so much because he was leaving her behind, as if he had to make the most of the time left. I wished and wished I didn't know anything at all, that some devil hadn't made me get up out of bed that night and listen. Because it's so much easier to be innocent. I'd eaten the M&Ms ages ago, and it seemed to me that they were like the fruit in the story of the Garden of Eden poor Grandma once told me – you know, that grew on the tree of knowledge. Being thirteen, and knowing things had brought me nothing but misery.

One day I decided to tell Mama that I knew. I couldn't keep it inside myself any longer. More than anything I wanted us to feel like a family once more, who shared things, good and bad. I decided that if I told Mama I could make things better. Maybe I could even persuade Tata to change his mind. Surely life couldn't be that bad for him – not when he loved Mama so much. I knew it was my duty to talk him out of going. Then we would have a lovely Christmas together, and everything would be all right.

It was a bitterly cold Saturday at the beginning of December, and Mama and I had been out to get our oil ration. She was in a good mood because we'd also bought some beetroot and some bacon and the ingredients for mamaliga – the old-fashioned corn mush dish her mother taught her to make, and which I loved.

"We'll have a feast this weekend, little Flo," she smiled.

The bags were heavy. We carried one each. I tucked my free hand in her free arm, and we walked slowly home, heavily muffled against the icy wind.

All the time I was wondering how I could raise the subject.

"Mama…" I began.

"Ugh, it's started to snow," she said. I looked up. A few small flakes were whirling down from the leaden sky, and I blinked as one went into my eye, stinging and cold.

"Let's take the short cut," said Mama, walking faster, "I really don't want to get colder than I already am."

There was a building site over the road. It seemed that half of the city was being knocked down and rebuilt, and where we lived was no exception. Instead of walking the long way round, on the main road, we would walk through the site despite the notices saying KEEP OUT. It was all right on a Saturday because the workmen weren't there.

All I could think of was how much I wanted to talk to her. In my mind I rehearsed my opening sentence.

Mama, I overheard you and Tata talking...

Mama, why does my father want to leave us...

Mama, I know Tata is going to try to escape and I want to talk to you about it...

Mama, why didn't you both tell me? Treat me like a person, not a child...?

"Please, Mama..." I began.

But she stopped suddenly, and her bag of shopping fell to the ground. Only the beetroot rolled out, stopping a few metres from our feet. My mother was gripping my arm so tightly it hurt, and I cried out.

"Oh my God ... oh my God," she whispered, staring straight ahead as if she had seen a ghost.

I looked.

It wasn't a ghost – it was something far more shocking. And (it took me a few seconds to realize) frightening. There, on a half-built concrete wall ahead of us, someone had daubed a slogan. The white paint ran down like tears. It said, "DOWN WITH CEAUŞESCU".

This was the wildest, wickedest, most dangerous thing – if you believed all we were told in school about our country and our leader. It was unimaginable. *Down with Ceauşescu.* A terrible crime, to daub that on a wall in a public place. It was unthinkable: yet there it was in front of us.

76

My mother began to shake. She was still gripping my arm fiercely, but looking all round, panic-stricken.

"Don't look! Don't see it!" she hissed.

I thought that was rather stupid, because how could I not see something that was before my eyes, in huge white letters?

"Quick, let's get out of here. Before someone sees us!" she cried.

"But Mama! We didn't put it there!" I said.

"Don't be stupid, Flora! We're HERE! We'd be accused!" she said, almost crying as she picked up the bag. "Come on!"

She started to rush away, not waiting for me. I hurried after her for a little way, then remembered something.

"Mama! The beetroot!"

"Leave it, Flora! Hurry!"

That was too much for me. I turned back, and ran to where the beetroot – promising wonderful bright red soup – lay like a dark crimson ball on the ground. I scooped it up quickly, and ran after her. But my heart was thumping, as my eyes were drawn again to that writing on the wall.

Who could have been so foolish?

Or so brave?

SIX

Of course, I never got the chance to have that conversation with my parents. Maybe if I had, things would have been different. I wouldn't have felt so lonely any more. I wouldn't have been driven...

When Mama and I got home, me clutching the precious beetroot as if my life depended on it, she sat down heavily in the chair as if she was going to faint. She looked strange — as if the skin was stretched tightly over the bones of her face, ghostly and pale.

"Rodika — what's the matter?" my father asked, in alarm.

She shook her head. He looked at me, and so I told him. His response was extraordinary. First he put his finger to his lips, and flapped the other hand, telling me to keep my voice down. The walls of our apartments were cheap and thin, and the front door fitted badly. Whenever my parents wanted to talk about something important they would put the radio on, so people in the next flat couldn't hear. But now I sounded very loud in the silence, saying "Down with Ceaușescu".

It took a second after that for what I'd said to sink in. Then he closed his eyes, threw back his head, and punched the air with one fist.

"Oh," he whispered, half to himself, "the fool! Whoever you are, I love you, you crazy fool! You dared!"

"Who, Tata?" I asked.

"How do I know? The man who painted that slogan on the wall, of course. They'll get him and he'll suffer. Oh, he'll suffer. But imagine the feeling of doing that. It would be worth the suffering."

"No, Constantin, NO!" My mother cried, in a strangled voice, dreadfully afraid.

He went across, and knelt at her feet, cradling her face between his hands and speaking tenderly. "Don't worry, darling," he said in a soothing voice, as if talking to a child, "I won't do anything like that. I couldn't. Too much is at stake. Please don't worry."

She bent forward and kissed him on the cheek — and I felt left out, as always. So I went into my bedroom, and shut the door.

On top of my little drawer unit sat my old doll, Mary. She was part of the furniture – something you stop noticing after a while, because it's always there. But something made me look at her now. She looked as if she had shifted position a bit. It was strange.

I stood looking at her for a moment, then picked her up and instinctively cradled her, just as I used to do. Alys had chosen the name, Mary – it was an English name, she said. I said, No; it was the name of the Virgin Mary, the Mother of Jesus. We weren't allowed to believe in those things. It was against the message of communism. But sometimes I found myself wondering about it all, and wishing there was such a thing as God. Not because I wanted to believe in him. Because I wanted to have someone to blame.

Mary was a sad old thing – an ugly plastic head with tatty blonde hair which had once been thick, but which I had brushed into patches of baldness. She had staring blue eyes, although, to be absolutely correct, only one worked; the other one had stuck shut, giving Mary a weird, winking look. Her eyelids had reached the same state of baldness as her head. Her body was made from once-pink cloth, now a dirty grey, and clad in a dark blue knitted dress my mother had made when I was four, and Mary was new.

Now she was old, battered, and perfectly hideous. But I'd loved her. Oh, how I had loved her!

I suppose I had loved her into ugliness.

Alys and I had little carts our fathers had made, and we would push our dolls around for hours. And we'd sit on the stairs and nurse them, singing lullabies and telling stories, and really believing that our dolls were real. When Tata used to tease me and call Mary a "doll", I used to go mad and put my finger to my lips, saying, "Shhhh."

"Don't be mean. You'll hurt her feelings," I'd say. "She isn't a doll. She's REAL!"

Then later, as I got older, I would lower my voice to a whisper, and cover Mary's ears with my hands, saying to my mother, "You see, she thinks she's real. She doesn't know she's just a doll..."

I smiled to remember it. It's funny the way children cling on to their beliefs for so long, keeping the real world at bay. Then the morning comes when you wake up, and you're hugging your beloved doll, and you feel the hard plastic head and the grubby cloth body – and suddenly you know that what you're loving IS just plastic and cloth. And you feel a bit of a fool to yourself, because you can't just throw the thing away. It's become a part of you.

Now my old doll reminded me of so many things I'd lost. Like Alys. And complete trust in my parents. And belief in ... what? Well, a sort of miracle, I suppose. That something obviously fake CAN be real at the same time, and worthy of your love.

I went to sit on the bed, gazing down at her sadly. She leered up at me, with her one horrid blue eye, and sealed pink eyelid. With my fingernail, I peeled a piece of red paint from her mouth. Then I felt guilty, wincing as if I had just picked a fresh scab. So I smoothed her patchy hair, to make her feel better.

Suddenly I wanted so much to believe again — to make everything like it was. Couldn't you make ugly things beautiful again? Couldn't you put things right, if you tried hard enough?

Without knowing quite why, I jumped up, pulled open my drawer, and took out my silky birthday gift. Folding it into a large double triangle, I wrapped it across the front of Mary's head, like a gypsy scarf, taking the ends round to the back of her neck, winding them tight, and bringing the wings forward over her shoulders. I crossed them over her chest, and tied the tips behind. A little tugging, and the old blue dress stretched down easily to cover her feet. Then I held her out to look at my handiwork.

All the patchy hair was concealed. So were her dirty-grey arms. She was swathed in brilliant red, black and green patterns, like a gypsy queen. All she needed now was a little surgery. So I took my old stylo pen, inserted the nib under the stuck eyelid, and worked at it carefully. After a few seconds I was able to prise the eyelid open – and Mary stared at me properly, with two blue eyes.

"Oh," I said, "you look much better!"

She was transformed.

She'd been given another chance.

Suddenly happy, I laid her carefully on my pillow – and decided in that instant to go out, and pay a call on Alys.

As I approached Alys's block, walking slowly because I felt a little nervous, wanting so much for Alys to want to be friends again, I saw a strange man slip around the corner of the building, and go in through the scratched swing doors. I stopped. He wore a big black overcoat, and there was something very shifty and suspicious about the way he had moved, as if afraid of being seen.

But then, I thought, *we're all like that. That's how it gets you in the end. You don't hold your head up, because it's safer to keep it down. Remember that proverb Tata used to quote? What was it? "The sword does not cut a lowered head." They used to say that centuries ago in Romania. So we've ALWAYS been afraid.*

Reassured, I moved forward again, thinking about Alys. I'd say how sorry I was we had fallen out. I'd ask her if she understood why it happened... No, I wouldn't. A waste of time, to talk about the past. I'd tell her ... I'd tell her I wouldn't spend any time with Daniel Ghiban, or Mariana, or Luminitsa – not any more. It would just be me and Alys again, just like it always was. And I could confess to her about Mary, knowing she'd understand.

I started to mount the stairs to the fourth floor, glad the climb wasn't as high as ours. There was the familiar smell of damp, paraffin, and boiling vegetables, which seemed to ooze from the walls of all these apartments. I was used to it. It was a part of life.

When I got to Alys's landing I paused. I could hear soft voices from her flat. That must mean her parents were in, and that pleased me. I'd always liked Mr and Mrs Grosu. They were older than my parents, but large and jolly. I wondered if Alys had told them about our falling-out ... but knew she must have done. She was close to her parents. They'd always treated her like a grown-up.

I knocked on the door, softly at first, then more loudly. The soft sound of conversation ceased. Then I heard quiet footsteps approach the front door.

"Who is it?" said a man's voice. It might have

84

been Mr Grosu, but I wasn't sure.

"Flora!" I called.

There was a silence. It seemed to go on for a long time. I began to feel uneasy – sensing something was wrong. Then there were more footsteps.

"Hello?" said a voice. Alys's voice.

"Alys – it's me, Flora!" I called.

But the door was not flung open as I expected. Instead there was another puzzling silence; then a whispering.

"Please open the door, Alys!" I called.

After a couple more minutes – minutes in which I began to feel horribly unsure of myself, and wished I had not come – the door was at last opened a crack. Alys's face peered out at me, white in the gloom.

"What?" she said.

"I ... I want to talk to you," I said.

"No," she said. Her eyes instinctively swivelled, as if someone was behind her.

"What's the matter?" I asked. "Can I come in?"

"No ... no, you can't," she said.

"But, I came... Oh, I need to talk..."

Eyes down, she shook her head fiercely.

It was as if some vile creature, a monster I couldn't have invented in my worst nightmares, was plucking at the flesh of my heart with long, sharp fingernails. I was hurting so much it was impossible for me to move.

So I blurted, "Please, Alys. I was playing with Mary ... and I was thinking ... remembering lots of things... Can you come out with me? I want to sort things out..."

Alys closed her eyes briefly, the way people do when they are so irritated they can't stand it any more. Then she stared at me, but she wasn't really looking at me at all. Her eyes were as blank and blue as Mary's. Yes, that was it. With her blonde hair slightly greasy around her forehead and those cold staring eyes, she was like a doll. Unreal.

"Look," she said, "I can't talk now. I don't... Oh, please just go away, Flora. *Go away!*"

I lost my temper then. It was as if all my unhappiness surged up like a swollen river and burst the walls of the dam. "I came to make friends, Alys Grosu," I yelled. "And you don't deserve it! You hear me? You don't deserve to have any friends! You're a horrible cow, and I shan't bother with you again – OK?"

With that, I couldn't stop myself, I kicked out furiously at her door – wanting it to catch her in the face, to teach her a lesson. In her shock she stepped back sharply, and the door flew open.

And before she had time to catch it and slam it

shut in my face I saw two men standing in the doorway of the living room, just behind her. One of them was her father. But the other one was the stranger in the long black coat I had seen slipping into the building ahead of me.

Blinded by tears I fled down the stairs, almost falling down the last four or five, only saving myself by clutching at the broken banister. When I rushed outside at last I could hardly breathe; my heart was thumping so strongly I thought it would burst from my chest. I leaned against the wall for five, ten, fifteen minutes … I don't know how long. It was only when the cold began to penetrate my jacket that I recovered, and slowly started to walk away.

All the suspicions of the last few weeks bubbled to the surface of my brain. Alys and her family had something to hide – otherwise why would she have behaved like that? Why would her father, listening, have let her treat me like an enemy? And that man … I allowed myself, now it was over, to whisper what he looked like. It was a word which chilled any Romanian, innocent or guilty.

Securitate.

The dreaded Secret Police.

I remembered my father saying to my mother that there was something about them – "you can almost smell them," he said, so in my upset state that is what I thought. I couldn't help it.

I could not go home. I knew Mama would look at me and know something had happened. And how could I tell her? It's a terrible feeling to know you have nobody to talk to – nobody in the world. It was like not having a home, not belonging anywhere.

So despite the small flurries of snow, and the icy wind, I made my way across the bleak wasteland, and walked in the direction of our school. It was just habit. I did that walk every day, and like a little lost animal, I was following a familiar route. My head was down. I hunched my shoulders against the cold.

When I reached the school at last I stopped, confused for a moment, not knowing quite what to do. The road was deserted; the school looked dead. For a few seconds I gazed at the cluster of modern buildings I knew so well, as if I had never seen them before. Grey, grey, grey. Everything was grey, and straight, and ugly. I found myself longing for some colour to enter my life, some fun, like I used to share with Alys.

I turned my back on the place, and crossed the road. Quite quickly I reached an older area, with nineteenth-century houses set back from the road, overgrown with ivy. They were very grand to me, these houses, although I knew that many of them were in fact divided into apartments. Wistfully I gazed through an iron railing into a wild garden, all overgrown and mysterious.

Suddenly I felt a tap on my shoulder. I drew in my breathe sharply, feeling the cold hit the back of my throat. *This is it*, I thought, *Alys has sent that man after me*... I was trembling with cold – and terror – as I turned round.

And there was Daniel Ghiban grinning at me. I couldn't believe it, and thought my legs would give way with the relief. So I put my hand on my chest and laughed.

"Phew!"

"Who'd you think it was? The President?"

"Oh yes – come to find me, to offer me a job running the schools!"

"No," he said, with mock-seriousness, "to say that you've been chosen to run the restaurant at the Intercontinental Hotel!"

"Chief cook and taster!" I said.

Feeling awkward now, I started to walk, and he fell into step beside me – quite easily – as if he had been intending to all along.

"What are you doing this way?" he asked.

"Just walking. I ... had to get out of the house.

You know the feeling? I didn't expect to meet anyone. What about you?"

"I live near here."

"Oh."

"Where are you going now?" he asked.

Suddenly I wanted to cry. I couldn't prevent my voice from wobbling, as I replied, "I … I don't know." The it slipped out, "I had a quarrel."

"Well … come with me!" he said brightly. "I think you need cheering up."

He started to stride, so that I had difficulty keeping up. But it didn't matter. I was relieved to be taken control of, to follow without asking questions. All that had happened so far that day had been too much for me. I needed to be led, to be looked after.

Daniel was wearing a vivid green scarf which stood out against the smart, dark blue of his anorak. His cheeks were red with cold. I thought he looked brilliant.

He turned right, and soon we were in a small park area I didn't recognize. The grass was covered with a light sprinkling of snow; the trees were like lace against the sky. Daniel bent down quickly, scooped up a handful of frosting, and scattered it over my hair.

"Diamonds!" he laughed.

"Pig!" I shouted, feeling the snow melt on my face, and bending to get my revenge. My handful fell short of its target, scattering on the air.

"You won't catch me, little squirt!"

He started to run, and I followed, knowing I didn't have much chance of catching a boy as athletic as Daniel. Alys would have caught him easily...

"If you catch up I'll give you a present," he yelled over his shoulder, running quite slowly ahead of me, but still too fast for me. Then he was weaving, and doing funny leaps, and generally behaving so ridiculously – all just out of reach – that I was helpless with laughter.

"Oh ... oh ... I've got to stop! My stomach hurts..." I puffed, between giggles.

"Truce?"

I nodded.

"OK then ... let's go and have a rest."

He led the way to a little shelter, open on three sides, and built in the style of a sort of peasant hut. I was warm now, from the running, and just wanted to sit down. When we were seated on the wooden bench, Daniel turned to me with a big smile.

"Now comes the cheering-up bit," he said.

"I'm already cheered up," I said.

"Well, this'll make you feel even better," he

said, putting his hand in his pocket. I heard a tantalizing rustle, and watched mesmerized as he drew out – a bar of chocolate!

It was Swiss milk chocolate.

I can see the wrapper now – pale blue, tucked neatly at the corners, with the word Lindt in lovely curly lettering.

I reached out a finger to touch it, and he smiled.

"Do you want to look at it for ever – or taste some?"

"Where did you get it?" I breathed.

"The usual."

"Don't tear the wrapper! I'd like to keep it," I cried.

Then followed the happiest forty or fifty minutes of my entire life. He divided up the chocolate equally, and I leaned back in bliss as it melted, smooth and creamy, in my mouth. We ate slowly, making each piece last. And as we ate we talked about many things. I told him about my chocolate island dream, and he told me that he always used to dream of flying off the top of a mountain, and floating through fluffy clouds. I told him about Mary, and he confessed that his favourite toy had been a teddy bear called Nicolas.

"I bet you don't have it now," I smiled.

"Somewhere in one of my cupboards – but don't

you dare tell the other boys," he grinned.

Then we talked about school and our favourite subjects, and what we wanted to be when we left school. I said I wanted to work in a museum or art gallery like my mother, because I liked the idea of all those precious things around, and being in charge of them. He said he would like to be a teacher in the University of Bucharest, which really impressed me.

That led the talk on to Mr Paroan and more painful matters at school. I don't know who mentioned Alys first, but I felt my face flame scarlet and tears fill my eyes. He asked me why I was upset, and his voice was so gentle and interested, it was as if all my terrible loneliness and confusion disappeared, melting like snow in watery winter sun.

So I told him how I had been thinking of the past, and wanting so much to be friends with Alys again. And what had happened when I got to her flat. As I remembered, the relief of talking was too much for me, and I started to sniff.

"I ... I ... just wanted a friend," I faltered. "It's ... it's been so awful at home. I've... I've... I've..."

"What, Flora?"

"I've been so un-hap-py," I cried.

"But why?"

I couldn't stop the tears. After all, they had been building up inside me, unshed, ever since I heard my parents talking about Tata's plan. Or was it before? It all merged into one now, and had to come out.

"They don't talk to me. I hate it. I hate their ... their secrets. It's not fair," I sobbed.

"*Shhhh, shhh*," he said, patting me on the shoulder. It was boyish and embarrassed, but he meant well, and I was glad of the human contact.

"What secrets?" he asked then.

I shook my head. "Nothing ... noth-ing."

"Won't you feel better if you tell somebody?" he asked. "It's not good to have things bottled up inside you."

Daniel's voice sounded like that of a man so much older – someone caring and wise. I knew in a flash he was right. And so I told him all the things that had been making me miserable, from the overheard rows that I didn't understand, until the awful night when I discovered the truth. I told him *everything*.

"And you see," I finished, "what makes it worse is I feel so guilty. I know I should be worrying about Tata getting caught or something. But instead I'm just angry with him for making the decision. It doesn't seem fair."

"It hurts you...?"

I nodded, unable to speak.

He had his hands clasped in his lap, and looked down at them, shaking his head. "I can see just how you feel," he said. "Anybody would feel hurt. It's very hard for you..."

He understood. The relief of telling made me lean back against the shelter and close my eyes. I knew I must look a mess, with a red nose and swollen eyes, but I didn't care. All that mattered was the knowledge that I wasn't all alone any more. There was someone to talk to – a friend who understood.

SEVEN

All that happened on a Sunday. On the Monday, in school, I felt that there was a new, secret bond between Daniel Ghiban and myself. Nothing needed to be said. We chatted about the usual things: teachers, school work, things we would like to own, or eat. Nothing important.

All that mattered were my own feelings. Even though nothing had really changed – my father was still bent on his mad plan; Alys was still a terrible worry – I felt better. At the centre of my mind, like a warm flame, was the relief of having confided in someone *and* the flattering feeling that the person thought me special. So it was *me, me, me*. I know that sounds selfish, but people can't help worrying about themselves. Looking back, of course, I hate myself. I think what a silly, self-centred little girl I was. Why wasn't I thinking more about my parents, and what they were going through? But you don't, do you? You are the centre of your own universe – until something happens to knock you off that pedestal.

An odd, quiet time followed, in which people stopped talking about Maryon and Mr Paroan, and just got on with their lives. There was a sense of Christmas approaching; we all chatted vaguely and wistfully about what our parents might buy us, knowing all the time it was likely to be little. But we had lots of tests in school too, which was boring – but useful too, in that they united us all in hating being forced to learn all that boring stuff. Dates. Formulae. Grammar. Names.

I wondered if, as well as having chocolate and bananas to eat, kids in the West had to suffer like this as well. They must. And I was actually rather glad!

At the back of my mind, though, was the Big Question.

WHEN?

When would Tata make his move?

My mother wondered too, I knew, because she grew very tense, as the weather got colder and colder, and we rolled into December. They didn't talk so much, although he still showed her plenty of affection. Just one little comment I overheard.

They were both in the kitchen, and thought I was in my bedroom, and he said to her bitterly, "You see, Rodi? The Wall comes down, and the Czechs and the Poles raise flags of freedom, and Hungary's borders are open, and even the Bulgarians have seen the light — but what about us? Not in a million years. Now do you see…?"

There was a silence, but she probably nodded. What else could she do but agree with him?

Not long after that, she got ill. It was nothing serious, just something a bit worse than a very bad cold, but it made her shiver and sweat, and she had to stay in bed. I felt so sorry for Mama, lying there with bright, feverish eyes, and her long dark hair in rats' tails round her face. She fretted that she couldn't go out to queue for food, and go to work, and cook, and do all the things she usually did. My father and I reassured her that we could cope.

"I'm thirteen now, Mama," I said. "That's almost grown up!"

So my life changed a bit. In the morning, (though it still felt like night) I got up over an hour earlier, wrapped myself up in as many layers of clothing as I could find, pulled my woollen hat well down over my eyes and ears, and went out into the freezing darkness to join a queue. My father did the same. We would walk out together in silence, really tired still and each longing to be in bed, and trudge to the shops, parting company to join different queues. My job was usually to get the bread.

When you've grown up with queues – waiting in line for absolutely everything – they become a part of your life, like the electricity supply going off and on, the lift not being finished, the roads having big holes in them, and so on. But now that I was taking my mother's place in the early morning, I noticed things I hadn't seen before. Like the silence of people. There's a long line of women (mostly women, but some men too) waiting outside a shop, their faces lit only by the pale blue light from the window, their shoulders hunched against the cold and their breath frosting in white clouds before their faces. They're all carrying shopping bags. And none of them are talking, even though they see each other every day. It's so strange, so unreal – this intense silence between neighbours, acquaintances – even friends.

But why?

It's more than people just being tired and gloomy, I thought one morning, as I stood there; conscious that Alys's mother stood two people in front of me, that she had seen me quite clearly, and turned her back. It's because nobody trusts anybody. If you're seen being friendly, it could be to the wrong person – and noticed by the wrong person. Or maybe it's just that people have forgotten the art of speech.

I would get to school more tired than ever, and it was twice as hard to concentrate on the lessons. Then, after school, I would start making supper, waiting for my father to come home, when he would take over.

My mother lay on the couch, her eyes big and shadowy in her white face. She called me over, and patted the place beside her. "Come and talk to me, Flora," she said. I did as she asked, and looked down at her, worried. I suddenly imaged her not getting better, tried to picture life without her, but the thought was too terrible and I thrust it away.

As if she read my mind she said, "Don't worry, I'll soon be better. I don't ache so much as I did yesterday. Tomorrow you can stay in bed and I'll go out for the bread."

I shook my head. "You will not," I said.

"It's hard for you, darling," she sighed.

"That's OK. We're all in it together!" I said, sounding as cheerful as possible.

She smiled. "In what?" she asked.

"The mud!" I joked. But it wasn't funny.

"Tell me about school," she said.

"Well, I came top in history, and..."

"Good girl! My clever girl..." She stroked my arm, and I felt very pleased.

But then she started to cough – a dry, hacking sound, that made her face go red and her eyes stand out. She couldn't stop; her whole body was racked.

She was fighting for breath, her hands flapping at the air like flippers – and I felt frightened. I ran to the kitchen to get her some water, but she couldn't swallow. So I just held her head and shoulders tightly, supporting her, until the attack stopped.

Then my father came home. I told him what had happened; he sat down where I had been and fussed over her, smoothing her forehead gently.

"I tried to get you some aspirins. But no luck," he said. "Still, look what Stefan sent you..." He reached inside his jacket and pulled out something wrapped in brown paper. He shook it excitedly, then pulled off the wrapping to reveal a small unlabelled bottle filled with golden-brown liquid.

"Smell!" he said, unscrewing the top.

She pulled a face.

"It's brandy!" he said.

"Smells like paraffin!" she wheezed.

"No – it'll make you feel better. Take a swig."

She did so, made an even worse face as it went down, coughed a little, then lay back smiling. "Strong stuff," she said. "You have some, Constantin. It'll do you good. I think you need it more than I do!"

That was when I stalked off into the kitchen feeling so irritated with my father. It was the same old story – she was thinking about him, even though she was ill, and he was making all this fuss and pretending to worry about her, when all the time he was going to leave us. It was all very well for that man Stefan to send some precious brandy, but he was going to take my father away – whether Mama was ill or not.

At last Tata came into the kitchen, humming as he took potatoes and salami out of his bag. I could smell the brandy on his breath. "I think that cheered her up," he said, in a quietly satisfied way.

Suddenly I couldn't bear it. I felt something give way inside me, and a sort of roaring in my head as my real feelings took control. I turned to him. "There's only one thing that would make her happy," I said angrily. "And that's for you to show you really care. It's no good just shoving a bottle of brandy under her nose. That won't last long – especially if you drink it! No – what about showing you really love her by staying with her? What about letting your friends get out on their own, and you staying to look after us? What about THAT then?"

My voice was loud in the silence. He said nothing, just stared at me with a frozen, shocked expression. Then I heard my mother's horrified voice from next door. "Shhhh," she hissed, then called in a loud whisper, "Flora! I want you to come here."

I went back into the living room, and he followed me, his head hanging, saying nothing. Mama was sitting up, looking gravely at us both. Then she pointed to the bed beside her, and spoke in that way which allows for no argument. "Sit down here again, Flora. And Constantin, you sit in the chair. It's obviously time we had a talk. Put the radio on."

When I sat down beside her she took my hand. It was trembling, and I wanted to cry. She saw it, and stroked me gently. "Now, come on, little one. You obviously overheard us talking, didn't you. When was it?"

"A long time ago. I don't remember," I whispered.

"You shouldn't eavesdrop. It's wrong," said my father quietly.

"Lots of things are wrong," I said bitterly.

On the radio, a woman's voice was whining about love to the sound of a guitar.

Mama's hands went on stroking mine, regular and comforting. "*Shhh, shhhh,*" she said, as if soothing a baby, "I think it's time I had my say here. So you've both got to listen. Understand?"

I nodded, and so did he.

"Good. Now, Flora, when you get older and you meet someone you love, and want to marry, do you know what that means? What it really means?" I shook my head. "Well, when you love someone you love the whole person. Because of what they are. You don't want to change them. If you wanted to change them you might as well be with somebody else. Do you follow that?" I nodded. "Well, I know your father's been unhappy for some time. He's been like somebody wanting to – to – *burst* with unhappiness. When we first met I so admired him for the things he believed in. You remember, Constantin?"

We both looked across at him, and he nodded, looking very unhappy.

"Tata always dreamed of freedom, Flora. Of living in a country where people's minds are free. It's not about *having* things, like nice food and nice clothes. It's about what you are – *who* you are – in here." She tapped her own chest. "So, let's just get it clear. I want you to understand. Your father wants to live the life he used to dream of. That's the kind of man he is. And I love the kind of man he is. Flora, I have to want him to find his dream, mustn't I?"

I had to nod.

"Listen, Flora," she said, speaking more urgently. "There are a lot of things you're too young to understand, but I want you to try. Yes − I was against the plan at first. But now I know that Tata has to do it. Otherwise he'll die inside. So we just have to be very brave."

"But what … what will happen to us?" I gasped.

"When he gets to Germany he'll become a refugee. Then we apply to follow him. They'll ask us lots of questions, and (she gripped my hand very tightly) it will be horrible, Flora. I'm not going to lie to you. Life will be worse for us, because they'll punish us because he's got out."

My father groaned at that, and buried his head in his hands.

She went on, "But you know something? I know it will be all right. In the end they'll let us go. And in five or six years' time, when you are leaving school in Germany − or maybe some-where else, who knows − and living in the kind of society we all want, then you'll be glad. You will, Flora!"

I hung my head. They were both looking at me

and I didn't know what to say. My mother had been so strong and wise: I felt I couldn't match her.

They were waiting. At last I said, very quietly, "I felt left out – because you hadn't told me. It was horrible."

My father came over and stood by me, one hand resting gently on my head. "I'm sorry, little Flora – we probably should have talked it through as a family. But people never do, you know? Men have escaped without telling their wives even. And boys without telling their parents."

"I heard of a woman who sent her only son away, with a friend," said Mama, shaking her head, "because she loved him so much she was prepared to lose him – to give him a better life. Can you imagine that?"

I shook my head.

"Funnily enough, I can, because once you start thinking about these things, you hate this country more and more – everything it stands for."

There was a part of me that still didn't understand properly. Not this hatred of our country. It was all I knew, and so how could I want to leave it, as they did. Yet I knew they were right. They had to be right – because they were my parents.

"I want you to be free, Flora," said Mama. "I dream of getting you out."

"Not without you, Mama," I said, quickly, squeezing her hand.

"We'll be together – don't worry," she smiled.

"All of us," said Tata.

Then he squatted down beside me. I studied his face from close up. He was handsome, my father – dark, like Mama, with high cheekbones and piercing brown eyes. Those eyes stared deeply into mine, as if they could read my soul.

"I think we should have trusted you, my darling," he said softly. "We should have talked to you more. Will you forgive us?" I nodded and he smiled. "I'm glad. And now we can spend the next week trying to be happy... Yes, it'll be just about a week, so be strong for your Mama, little Flora. We can be really close now, can't we? But it's just us three – you understand? Nobody else in the world must know – are you really clear about that? *Not a soul!*"

I nodded, avoiding his eyes.

EIGHT

The next day Alys was absent from school, but it wasn't that which bothered me. It was Daniel Ghiban. He was deep in conversation with Mariana, and when I went up to say hello, he greeted me absentmindedly, as though I were a stranger. Then he seemed to turn his back, although it could have been my imagination. That's what I made myself think.

I tried to look carefree, but I was deeply hurt. All through the day it was the same. There was a wall of glass all round Daniel, setting him apart from me. He hung around with Mariana and Luminitsa and one or two of the boys, and (in truth) I felt very left out – and jealous.

I remembered the taste of the Swiss milk chocolate, and the sense of him beside me, listening so sympathetically ... and I could not believe the change. It worried me, for at the back of my mind my father's voice chimed: "*Nobody else in the world must know.*" I tried to forget it, but could not.

I tried to get through school as if nothing was wrong. My mother always used to tell me to hide my feelings in public: "Never let them know," she used to say. It was good advice and served me well that unhappy day.

When I got home, letting myself quietly into the flat, Mama was fast asleep. She looked better though, sleeping peacefully. I stood looking down at her for a few minutes, imagining what it would be like if she were to die, and feeling that inevitable choking inside. I don't know why I do that – deliberately making myself miserable. Maybe it's a way of testing your love for your parents: just imagining them not there is like looking into a terrible dark chasm. Imagine being that alone...

"Love you, Mama," I whispered. She stirred, but went on sleeping.

I sat down to make a start on my homework. The flat seemed very quiet, and I found myself looking forward to my father's arrival. I didn't have much time left with him and wanted to make the most of it.

A little later, there was a rap on the front door – a sharp, urgent sound. Afraid it would wake my mother, I darted quickly into the hall, shutting the door behind me. The rap came again. For a second I wondered if Tata had forgotten his key, but that never happened. Then I realized that it might be a stranger, and since Mama was so sound asleep it was as if I was alone. So I certainly shouldn't open the door. Another rap, then another, even louder.

I opened the door a crack, peering out into the gloom of the landing.

"Quick!" said a voice I knew well.

Alys stepped forward, pushing past me, and closing the door. I stared. Her chest heaved, as though she had run up the stairs two at a time. With blonde hair stuck to her forehead, and a wild, drawn face, she looked exhausted and terrified.

"Alys! What...?" I began.

"Oh my God, Flora! Oh God!" she panted.

"What's wrong?" I cried, putting out a hand to steady myself against the wall, as if I knew in advance that what she had to say would make the whole place spin.

"We have to warn him ... your father! We have to find him — now!"

She put out a hand and gripped my arm tightly. For a second or two I wasn't able to speak. I simply stared at her, my mouth open. Then I croaked, "Tell me!"

Alys was panting less; maybe the sight of my fear and confusion calmed her down, and she realized she had to take charge. "Listen carefully," she said in a low, intense voice, "They're going to pick your father up. There's a man downstairs already, waiting for him – and another one in a black car out on the road. So somehow or other we have to get to him before he reaches the estate. You know the way he comes?"

I nodded. "But ... but ... why? I don't understand! What's happened?"

Alys's face was hard. "Oh, Flora, it's partly my fault. I tried to warn you but ... oh, it's too much to go into now. I'll explain everything later ... if I can. But ... oh Flora, you were such a fool. Daniel Ghiban..."

When she said that name I really did feel sick and faint. I knew (as if it had been written in a book I had had in front of me for weeks but been unable to read) what she was about to say. As if from a distance I heard my own voice whisper, "What?"

"All that stuff about his mother and the British Embassy! He's bad, Flora! I knew he was. His father's no porter – he's *Securitate!*"

"How ... how do you know?" I gasped.

"Too long to tell... Just believe me, Flora!"

"Mr Paroan? And Maryon?"

She nodded.

"Never mind about all that now… We've got to save your father. If we get to him when he comes out of the Underground…"

"Did the man downstairs see you come in?" I asked.

She shrugged. "It's dark, and I had my hood up. Some other people were coming in, and anyway, he wasn't looking out for me. Oh, come on!"

I grabbed my dark jacket, reached for my light blue knitted hat, hesitated – then chose the old black woollen hat that hung in the hall for anyone to use. We closed the door gently behind us and, treading very quietly, began the long walk downstairs. In the dim light from the low bulbs on every half-landing, I could see Alys ahead of me, dark and shapeless with her hood covering her hair once more. Once she looked back, as if to check I was following, and gave me a small smile of encouragement. Just like the old Alys.

When we reached the bottom, she took my arm and drew me into the shadows.

"He'll probably know what you look like," she whispered.

"But how?" I breathed.

"They know everything. Well … almost everything," she replied.

"What shall we do?" I asked.

"Didn't some people move out from this floor last week?"

"Yes…"

"Come on then!"

There were four flats on the ground floor. I had forgotten that one of them was newly empty. It didn't occur to me to worry about the door being locked.

We crept along the corridor, and halted outside the end flat, Number Four. Alys put her shoulder to the door and pushed. She was very strong, and the doors to all the flats were cheap and flimsy. A man, attacking the door with his shoulder, would certainly break the lock – but not a thirteen-year-old girl.

"It's hopeless," I groaned.

"Wait!"

I had underestimated Alys all along, and this was no exception. She was fumbling in her pocket; in the poor light I couldn't see what she brought out, but heard a regular clicking and scraping. Then I realized. It was the precious old penknife she carried everywhere, and which we all used to borrow in school to sharpen our pencils.

That is until Daniel Ghiban arrived, with his smart metal pencil sharpener. I began to shiver.

"Hurry, Alys!"

She was pushing and prising, putting all her weight to the small blade as she slid it down between the doorpost and the door, again and again. At last there was a small splintering sound, and she heaved, and the knife blade broke – just as the lock gave way.

Inside it was pitch dark, but that didn't matter, because all the flats had a similar layout. We groped with our hands, searching for a door into the living room. Once inside we could see a little, in the glimmer of light from the window that opened onto the side of the block.

Alys was across the room in a minute, tugging at the window catch. Once she'd got it open, she held out her hand to me. "Quick – you go first. I'll hold your hands and lower you down."

Because of the steps at the entrance, the ground floor was raised: about a three metre drop to the hard earth. I clambered up and turned round so that I was kneeling with my back to the outside. Then I started to lower myself down, Alys taking both my hands at last – and my full weight – so that I was suspended by her until I dropped. She followed quickly, swinging from the sill easily before letting herself go.

"OK? We don't want any sprained ankles!" she whispered.

"Let's go," I said.

There was only one snag to this plan. We were at the side of the block; the *Securitate* man was waiting at the front. Yet to go anywhere we had to cross the waste ground, because our block was at the very edge of the development, only a high wall behind. The four blocks were placed rather like the legs of a table, with the wall running all the way round, and a metal barrier at the entrance. It was, as Tata always said, rather like a prison.

So all we could do was to creep across the stretch of ground between our block and the neighbouring one, then pretend we had come out of that entrance, and walk out in front, making for the barrier.

The blocks were close, but it seemed quite a long way across, and I felt that each lighted window was an eye, watching. Although we were almost invisible in our dark clothes I imagined everybody must be able to see us, and any second someone would throw open a window and shout a challenge.

At last we reached the next block, and walked along the side until we reached the front. We stood for a few minutes, plucking up courage to walk out to where the waste land was lit by dull yellow lamps. I was sure the thudding of my heart must arouse the whole neighbourhood.

"Let's go!" Alys whispered.

We detached ourselves from the shelter of the building, and strolled out into the open. I wanted to look round, but didn't – just kept on walking, concentrating on appearing relaxed. It was very hard. I wanted to run, and quickened my pace. So did Alys. I could feel eyes watching and felt that we MUST look obvious. But there was nothing else to do but walk on, making for the metal barrier.

Beyond it was the road – and the black car.

"I'm so scared," I muttered, through chattering teeth.

"Listen," said Alys, "if they chase us you've got to get away. You've got to find your father. You'll have to leave them to me."

"Don't be silly!" I cried.

"You must," she said.

Ahead of us we could see the entrance – the one-and-a-half metre metal barrier that would only be raised to let in a car, but no one I knew had one. It was illuminated by harsh yellow overhead lights – just there, just at the entrance. The development became progressively darker away from the road. At this moment I longed for a universal power failure – for the safe darkness that would cover our departure.

I felt very small. The place was deserted: we were the only things moving on that bleak December evening. Every second I expected to hear a shout from behind us, and the sound of running feet but there was nothing. As we grew nearer and nearer to the barrier I thought of my father coming nearer and nearer home and had to control my muscles to stop myself breaking into a panicky run.

I could see the car – about twenty metres off now.

"Keep walking," muttered Alys, "and keep your head down."

But I couldn't help staring ahead.

And I saw, as if in slow motion, the car door open, and a man get out. He stood there for a few seconds, staring at us. We kept walking. Then he began to move too, towards us – with only the barrier in between.

I'll never know if he recognized me or not. All I know is that I felt a moment of such terror, it made me stop in mid-stride, and half-turn, as if to run. It was a big mistake, for men like that are trained to interpret the slightest suspicious movement. He yelled, "You! Stop!"

Then everything happened at once. Alys's hand shot out, and she gripped my arm so there was no escaping. "Run, Flora!" she shouted, setting off and dragging me with her – but *towards the man*!

As we pounded along she just had time to pant her instructions. "Don't slow down… When we get there you duck underneath ... don't stop whatever happens ... just think about your father ... don't think about me..."

We were nearly at the barrier. The *Securitate* man was standing square in front of us, waiting. Then Alys did something I shall never forget. We were just a few metres away from the barrier, when she let go of me, shot ahead, and leapt. One hand on the top of the barrier, her whole weight swinging sideways with beautiful athletic speed, legs firmly together, and *crash* – the momentum of her brilliant vault took her heavy feet straight into his face.

I was dimly aware of him staggering back and falling, and Alys's voice screaming, "Go, Flora! Go!" And like a little hunted animal I darted under the barrier, and ran and ran. There was no time to wonder what was happening behind me. With the blood pounding in my head, my whole body straining to move faster than it had ever done, and the bitter air burning the back of my throat as I struggled for breath, I was beyond all thought, even all fear. Alys and I had ceased to matter. *Tata* ... *Tata* ... *Tata* ... *Tata* ... drummed the rhythm of my whole body.

Of course, I knew the way he always came home. It wasn't a direct route from the Underground; he always made a detour along a narrow side road

where there were a few shops, and where sometimes one or two country people came to sell a few
turnips or (if you were lucky) apples. We went
there to shop. I reached it and ran down the street,
oblivious to the stares of passers by. And as I came
to the end I saw Tata just turning.

Too breathless now even to yell, I ran up to him.
My face must have been white; he stared at me in
utter astonishment. Dragging him by the arm I
pulled and pushed him back the way he had come.
He realized that something was clearly very wrong
and fell into step beside me without any protest. As
we ran back towards the large black entrance to the
Underground, gaping in the street like the mouth
of Hell, I managed to pant out an explanation.

But I only warned him they were waiting for
him. I only told him they had been tipped off. I
didn't tell him about Daniel Ghiban. I didn't confess that it was all my fault.

"Tata ... you've got to hide," I gasped.

We were at the top of the Underground steps. I
thought I heard someone shout, some way behind
us. Quickly we ran down and down, pushing past
people, not caring how much they stared and
protested. Through the gloomy tunnel we ran, our
footsteps echoing like an army of people, running
for their lives.

Then we were on the platform. For a moment I glanced at the dull silver of the rails, stretching into blackness each way, and thought what a relief it would be to jump down onto those rails and end this terror, and the agonizing pain in my ribs. But the thought disappeared as soon as it came. Like so many people in terrible circumstances I realized how strong is the will to survive. Because in your heart you believe, you really do believe, that everything will be all right in the end.

I heard the rumble of a train. "Take me with you, Tata," I begged.

"No, little Flora," he said grimly, flinging an arm around my shoulders and pulling me to him. "You'll be safer away from me."

"I want to be with you," I cried.

"You must look after your mother for me. Do you hear me, Flora? Look after Mama!"

Then there was the regular flash, flash, flash of lighted windows as the train pulled in with a roar. The doors slid open, a few people got out, there was a last, fiercely loving pressure on my shoulders, then I was alone on the platform. The next second, the door crashed shut in front of my father's frightened face, and the train rumbled off in the darkness, taking him away.

NINE

Stunned by grief, I made my way slowly back home, not knowing what I would find. And it was so strange, so unreal ... the fact that there was nothing to be seen. It was as if nothing had happened. No car, no Alys, no man outside the entrance to the block – nothing. All wiped off the face of the earth.

But when I reached our own front door I heard voices inside. One rough and angry, the other weak, yet defiant. When I entered the living room Mama was standing face to face with a thickset man in a black leather jacket.

"Well, what have we here?" he said unpleasantly, as I stood looking at him.

"Leave the child alone," said my mother, clutching her dressing gown around her. She was pale.

"Do you know where your father is?" he demanded, ignoring her.

I shook my head, deliberately looking stupid.

"Why should she know?" asked my mother.

If she was afraid, she didn't reveal it at all. And I knew I mustn't show my own fear. Men like this might be brutal, but they weren't necessarily clever. The only chance was to keep calm and bluff.

"I'm sorry I'm late, Mama," I said.

"Where've you been?" asked the man, suspiciously. But my heart gave a little skip at that. He didn't know. The other one must have chased Alys.

"Oh, I had to do some jobs after school," I said vaguely.

"Good girl," said Mama, calmly.

He looked at us, his cold gaze moving from one to the other, then back again. Then he asked, "Did your husband tell you of his plans?"

"Of course not!" said Mama, "Do you tell your wife about your plans? I never knew a man who told his wife anything!"

"You're not a very good liar," he said.

"No – and that's why I always tell the truth," she replied quickly.

I went across to stand by my mother, slipping my arm around her waist. Her dressing gown was wet through with sweat. And I felt her trembling as if she might fall.

"What are you doing here?" I asked.

"Waiting for your father," he said.

"You can't wait here," said my mother — and this time, I could hear the first note of panic in her voice. She began to cough again.

"My mother's been very ill. You'll get all her germs. So why don't you wait downstairs?" I said. At that I felt her stiffen, as if in protest. But I dug my fingers into her flesh, as if to tell her to be strong.

"Please go," I repeated, "my mother's got to lie down."

He hesitated, then lit a cigarette, blowing smoke in my mother's face. Her coughing was deafening now as it racked her whole body. "Well," he said, "I won't be far away. Don't try anything, because there's nothing you can do. He knows that too." And with a mocking nod he turned and left the flat.

I ran across the room, switched on the radio and I told her all that had happened. She burst into helpless tears. She had to muffle the sound by burying her face in the pillow. "Oh, Constantin ... my Constantin," she sobbed.

"At least he got away, Mama!"

"That's thanks to you and Alys," she whispered.

"I wonder what happened to her?" I said miserably. "They might have arrested her!"

And all we could do was cling to each other helplessly, crying quietly. Neither of us believed that anything would be right ever again.

When at last I went to bed I looked at Mary, then slowly removed her finery. She would remain plain, I thought, because that was the truth. For I'd been taken in by glamour and deceit. What Daniel Ghiban had turned out to be was far uglier than my poor doll. Guilty and full of grief, I put the scarf around my neck, and vowed to wear it every day until I saw my father again.

It was ten days before Mama was allowed to leave the flat. And I was ordered not to go to school. Always there was a man on duty downstairs – a rota of three different faces, all of them horrible-looking. It was a sort of informal house-arrest, only there was no charge, and there was no one to whom we could complain. I did my best to get us food. We lived on bottled cabbage, stale bread, pickled gherkins, cheap, fatty sausage, and potatoes. And all the time I worried about Mama never getting better. My father's absence affected her very deeply; it was as if she had forgotten how to smile. As if she felt there was no point in going on living.

Then, one day, there was a knock on the door, and there was Alys. I hadn't dared to go anywhere near her block but I felt we'd have heard if there had been trouble. Still, I was longing to know what happened after her spectacular, chin-smashing vault.

At last she was able to tell us. And when she saw the astonishment on my face, she grinned, "Somebody up there pulled the ghoul off your doorway," she said cheerfully. "Sorry it's taken me so long to come round, but I didn't think it would be wise."

"Oh, Alys!" I cried, and gave her a huge hug, joined by my mother, so that in the end she protested cheerfully that she couldn't breathe, and made funny flapping movements to wave us off.

When we were sitting down, she began her story, starting with the end. "I got him right in the face," she said with delight, "and while he was still wondering what hit him, I was off. I went the opposite way to you, Flora, thinking that they'd have to choose which one to follow. He chased me – he was yelling! Really mad! But how could he catch me – stupid, fat old man!"

"You were very brave, Alys," said Mama quietly.

"No, he didn't have a chance," said Alys dismissively. "It was Flora who showed how well she could run."

I told her how I'd met Tata, and then we fell silent for a few seconds, thinking about him.

"I didn't tell him," I said at last in a small voice,

"about Daniel Ghiban. Oh, Alys I…"

"Flora, you…" she began at the same time, and then we both stopped. Mama looked puzzled, but I didn't want to explain. I needed to hear Alys's story.

"Tell me," I said.

She explained how she had been suspicious of Daniel from the beginning, with no proof. But then, (she took a deep breath at this point) her parents had taken her into their confidence at last, and she had learnt that her father was a part of an underground movement committed to rising up against Ceauşescu. They had started daubing "Down with Ceauşescu" on walls around the city. With contacts everywhere, they had discovered that Daniel Ghiban's father was an important man in the secret police.

"That day I came to your flat!" I cried, remembering.

"My father was having a meeting," she explained, "and I felt awful – but how could I let you in? How could we trust you?"

She said sadly that she couldn't have explained at that point. We both knew how much could have been avoided if only she had. My mother knew it too. She sat with her head in her hands, looking tired and sad.

"Ghiban made me suspect *you*," I said.

"You didn't believe him!"

"You don't know what to believe, when you're confused."

"That's the way these people work," said Mama. "They pour poison all over the place, knowing that sooner or later it's bound to kill somebody."

"Why did you trust him, Flora?" asked Alys.

I was silent – ashamed. I knew it was because of many different things: my need for flattery, my weakness for good things like chocolate, my feeling of being cut off from my parents, my longing for friendship. And yet, and yet... Weren't all those things perfectly normal? You could have scratched the surface of any of my classmates, and found similar truths.

As if she read my mind, Alys murmured, "Maryon trusted him too."

"Poor Maryon," said my mother. "But what about the teacher?"

Alys shrugged. "My father thinks maybe Maryon told Daniel something about Mr Paroan. Or else he just followed him one day, and saw something ... I suppose we'll never know'

"But Daniel seemed so ... so ... *nice!*" I burst out.

"Flora, Flora, you should know better," said Mama softly. "Can you trust what people look like?

All over the world there are murderers who look like good neighbours, and good people who look ugly."

"But Daniel! *Why* did he do that?"

"If I was feeling kind I'd say he had no choice," said Alys sternly. "He's just a true son of his father, who's a true servant of Ceauşescu. And so it goes on. Anyway, he got well rewarded for informing, didn't he?"

I hung my head again. If Daniel Ghiban had walked into our flat at that moment, I swear I'd have jumped up and hit him, and kicked him, and paid him back for everything he had done. *No choice?* Was that really true? Could people get off that easily? When soldiers kill little children, and their mothers, is it enough of an excuse to say they were obeying orders, and had no choice? NO, I thought, *if you don't take the responsibility for what you do you might as well be a robot, not a human being.* Yet I knew how wrong I had been too...

And somewhere within me a small voice was asking if Daniel Ghiban ever hesitated. If he ever felt a flicker of doubt because he really did like me. I hoped so. But we would never know that either.

"I wonder where Constantin is?" said my mother, half to herself.

"My father's asked people he knows. They say his two friends have disappeared too," said Alys.

"They might have been picked up," said Mama. "But at least I've got some hope. Maybe they crossed the border right away."

She sounded so sad I couldn't bear it. I ran across and flung my arms around her. "He'll get in touch with us soon, somehow or other — I know it! We've got to have faith, Mama!"

That was the chink of light in the black period. You have to believe in the people you love. And you have to believe in history too — that just around the corner there is a shift, which will take you off in a direction you never dreamt of.

Just two days later people were fired on in Timisoara, in the west of our country. It began with a humble priest — that's all. He was called Laszlo Tokes, a Hungarian, and when the people in charge tried to kick him out of his job, all the people who supported him took to the streets. It spread and spread — all the people's hatred of Ceauşescu, and all the years of oppression — coming to the surface at last. Some of them, including children, were killed by troops. And really, it was the beginning of the end for the dictator who had ruled our country for so long.

Of course, at the time my mother and I knew nothing of this. We were still being watched, although not for twenty-four hours a day any more. In a way we chose to remain prisoners in our flat, only going out to try to get food. My mother was sure some message would come from my father and she was determined to be at home when it did. The cold December days dragged on towards the year's end. We had no thought of any celebrations.

Early on the morning of 21 December, coming back in the darkness with the usual unappetizing loaf, I saw two bulky, muffled figures ahead of me. Nothing could disguise Alys's loping walk; I ran to catch up. They swung round, startled by the sound of my feet, then visibly relaxed.

"Don't DO that!" said Mrs Grosu, quite crossly.

"It's OK, Flora – we're a bit…" Alys started to explain, looking at me apologetically.

Alys didn't finish. We walked on in silence for a while, until we reached the outside of our estate. Then Mrs Grosu stopped and looked up and down, really anxious. "Is the policeman still outside your place, Flora?" she asked.

"Most of the time," I replied. "But he wasn't there when I left. I think they're losing interest."

"Still, we shouldn't be seen together…"

"Oh, Mama!" Alys protested.

"You know why!" said her mother, "Come on, Alys!"

She strode ahead. Although I would have liked Alys's mother to be more friendly, I knew she was strained. We all were.

But before she ran to follow, Alys grabbed my arm, and put her mouth close to my ear. "Something's going to happen," she hissed. "They say I have to stay in the flat, for safety – but I'm not going to. Meet me…"

"Alys! Come on!"

I could barely hear what she said as she sped away. Yet in that moment I knew I would follow Alys wherever she led, and whatever happened.

My mother was up when I got back to the flat. We had some tea, and bread with Hungarian apricot jam. She announced that she felt so well she was going to clean the flat from top to bottom, and asked if I would help. I hesitated, trying to think of an excuse.

"I'm going out with Alys," I mumbled. "She … I … er… She said there's a peasants' market. We thought we'd see what we can find. Maybe some eggs!"

"All right, dear," she said. I felt guilty at the lie. An hour later Alys and I were on the bus, heading for the city centre. She had been very edgy, sending me ahead to the bus stop, whilst she hid around a corner. "Just make sure my parents aren't there.

Something might have delayed them."

"What do you mean? Where've they gone?" I asked, when I got back. She just shook her head, looking over her shoulder. "Wait and see," she said.

As we clung to the straps on the crowded bus, I could stand it no longer. "Where are we getting off?" I asked.

"Near Palace Square," she said, in a normal voice, "There's a big rally today."

I gaped at her. Palace Square was where the Party Headquarters was, with the balcony from which Ceauşescu spoke at special rallies. Usually these crowds were specially packed with supporters who would cheer him, and the rest were workers and students and even schoolchildren who had no choice but to be there.

"My parents have gone on ahead," Alys said, with a queer little smile.

The people on the bus seemed even more silent than usual. I looked about, knowing we could be heard, then back at Alys.

"WHAT?" I hissed.

"Yes – we're going to cheer Comrade President," she said.

TEN

There were hundreds of people streaming into Palace Square. Strangely, it was not as cold as usual, and so you could see people's faces without the usual mufflers up to the eyes. There was an odd atmosphere of tension. Perhaps it was because I was so astonished by this expedition, and frustrated by the way Alys just raised a finger to her lips and said, "*Shhhh*," when (once off the bus) I begged her to explain.

"Just keep your eyes open for my parents," she said tersely. "They'll kill me if they see me here."

It would have been impossible to find anyone in such a crowd. Thousands and thousands of people, many carrying banners and photographs of the President, crammed the square. There were buildings all round, making a kind of box, so that as the pressure of people grew I thought I'd be squashed.

There were no other children around us today. Usually they'd be ranged at the front, where they would sing their carefully learnt songs praising "mother and father" Nicolae and Elena, right in front of the Party Headquarters.

That was some way ahead of us, on the other side of the square. "I can't see a thing," I shouted at Alys, still wondering why on earth we were here.

"This way," she called, pulling me by my hand, and forcing her way through the people.

The next thing I knew, we were being pressed up against a lamppost. Someone had put some boxes around it, so it made a little raised island in the sea of people. And it was already occupied: about four young men, all about eighteen years old, clung on, staring intently ahead at the Party Headquarters.

"Hey! Let's get up there too – you're all taller than us!" called Alys cheekily, yanking one of the boys by the leg. He was tall and thin, with a pale freckled face, and carroty hair.

"You should be at home, little girls," he said, looking down without smiling.

"Oh, let them get up," said his friend, a cheerful-looking guy, wearing a blue peaked cap. He held out a hand. Alys grabbed it. Then the one who had first spoken jumped down in irritation, as we clambered up. Alys winked at me, and called down to him, "Thanks for making room for us!" From this vantage point I could see all round the square. Already the obedient ones at the front had started their cheers, calling "CEAUŞESCU ... CEAUŞESCU!" The banners and flags waved like washing. All eyes were fixed on the long balcony where the leader would appear.

At last he did. As you would expect, a cheer went up from the front of the crowd, but ... I looked around, surprised. There was a strange, heavy silence all around where we were standing, like the moment before a storm crashes through the heavens. Ceausescu's amplified voice echoed in this silence, crackling and unreal. I could see his tiny figure, his wife next to him, surrounded by men in dark overcoats, and wondered what he was saying. Something about his gratitude to the Bucharest Communist Party Committee for organizing this spontaneous rally. And going on to praise something called "scientific socialism"...

Then I heard it. A voice very near us said quietly, "Why don't you go home, you pig?"

It wasn't a shout – more like the sort of murmur you make in school, when you know there's no danger of the teacher hearing. I looked down, but all I could see were heads, all looking towards the balcony.

A foot stamped, and then another, but it was winter, and feet get cold standing still, and so that was normal. Yet I thought I heard a murmuring too, a soft sound, almost impossible to make out, which whispered things like, "Oh, shut up... We've listened to you for long enough... Get down!" I knew that was impossible, so I refused to believe what my own ears were telling me.

Then somebody hissed, right in my ear. I didn't dare look round, but knew it must have been the nice boy in the peaked cap who had pulled me up. The thin, snake-like sound was repeated, then taken up by another voice, then another, until all around us this little wind of rebellion, of contempt, of change, blew away the words of the President.

People started to boo; quietly at first, and then more loudly. But Ceauşescu carried on, even though soon his voice was drowned by the boos, the hisses, the shouts from the people in the square. I was staring. I heard Alys say, "It's happening!" but still could not believe what I saw. Ceauşescu, the President whom we had all been brought up to believe was perfect, like a god, had faltered. He looked shrunken and old, utterly confused by what he saw in front of him. In panic he waved one hand in front of him, as if trying to shoo away a troublesome fly.

But this fly wouldn't be chased off that easily. This fly was a big, stinging creature that wanted to taste his blood.

From the moment he faltered, confidence grew. I saw people shielding their faces, afraid they were being filmed by the secret police, and yet still yelling at the tops of their voices, "DOWN WITH CEAUŞESCU." Near us swelled the chant, "TIM-IS-OAR-A! TIM-IS-OAR-A!" in memory of those who had already died. And as the noise grew deafening, gradually all the faces looked up, as people who had lived for years in silence found their true voice at last.

Somebody grabbed Ceauşescu's photograph from a banner. The man carrying the banner tried to stop it happening, but was surrounded by jeering people. The picture was ripped up – then another – then another. I simply couldn't believe it.

Yet the noise in my ears was real enough. It was Alys, yelling and screaming and sometimes laughing hysterically, one arm holding on to the post, and the other one waving in the air.

"Look!" she shouted.

On the balcony the men behind the President were scurrying away. Only Ceauşescu and his wife were left, the old man still droning on about a pathetic pay rise he was going to give. I laughed. It was a bit late for that. It was all over. He berated "foreign imperialists". Then his wife's voice squawked over the loudspeakers, asking people to stay calm. Calm! When they suddenly saw an end to the oppression they had suffered for years and years and years! Who could stay calm?

The boy in the peaked cap jumped down, his face alight. So did his friends. "Let's go!" someone was yelling. "Let's take over the streets!"

They began to move away, then the one in the cap stopped, stepped back and looked up at us. "Go home now, girls," he said. "You've seen it. We've all seen it! But it'll get nasty now. So go home." Then he ran off.

I looked at Alys. Reading my mind, she shook her head. "I'm not going anywhere," she said stubbornly. "I want to see what happens. Anyway, Flora, my mother and father are somewhere in this crowd, and where they are ... that's home to me!" She thought for a moment, then added, "Who knows – your father might be somewhere here as well."

The crowd heaved around us. I looked desperately around at the faces, wondering if she was right. Then I turned back and looked her full in the face. "Did you know?" I asked.

"I knew something would happen," she replied, "because it was planned. That's why Mama was so tense, and why they ordered me to stay at home. But it could have gone wrong. People could have lost their nerve."

Most of the people stayed where they were. Soon helicopters whirred overhead like big, angry birds. People shook their fists, and uttered piercing whistles in protest. And a new cry went up, "No violence! No violence!"

At last Alys dug me in the ribs and we jumped down. I followed her, and I knew I had to do as she said, whatever happened.

There was a great surge of people out of the square, and we were carried along, unable to help ourselves. It was like being transported through time – from one moment of history into the next – being part of it without being able to do anything about it. People around us were responding in different ways. Some were shouting slogans against Ceauşescu and the Communist Party. Some were crying tears of joy. Some were silent and afraid, heads down, just running with the crowd like animals in a herd. When a group of soldiers appeared ahead of us, the crowd parting around them in fear, people cried out, "Don't fire on us! Don't use your weapons against us! We are the same people as you! You're young – don't kill young people for the sake of the old tyrant!" And so on.

Those soldiers didn't shoot. Their faces – very young all of them – were white, like masks. It must have been like a nightmare for them. As if you were a shepherd and suddenly all your sheep refused to obey, turning round instead to argue with you. You wouldn't believe it.

The soldiers didn't believe it.

In truth – I still didn't believe it.

It's amazing that when really dramatic things are happening your mind moves on a higher plane, and all your normal complaints are forgotten. Alys and I stayed on the streets for hours; yet at no time did we feel hungry, or cold, or tired. We watched men overturning cars, and painting anti-Ceauşescu slogans on walls, and burning photographs of the President and his wife. We saw people dragging the Romanian flag along, and hacking the Communist hammer and sickle symbol from the middle, then proudly waving the new flag, with its jagged gaping hole. Watchers cheered and clapped, and some bent to kiss this new symbol of freedom. Strangers clasped each other, weeping and calling each other "brother" and "sister". Old men and women ran along with the agility of people half their ages. Young men rampaged along, calling, "Don't go home! Stay on the streets! Make the revolution happen!"

At last it began to grow dark, and the clatter of the helicopters became more ominous. We were in Boulevard Balescu; the pressure of the crowd was immense. There must have been tens of thousands of people; if you closed your eyes you could hear the continuous low roaring, like waves on a shore. Ahead, I could see a line of militia men, wearing riot helmets and green overalls, weapons at the ready.

I think that was the first time I felt fear, and wanted to go home to my mother. But how could I? It was impossible to move in this crowd. So I held tightly to Alys's hand, and tried to take deep breaths.

It was then that we heard the first shots. The effect on the crowd was terrible; people started to panic and try to run in different directions. But there was nowhere to run. "Don't be afraid! Stand your ground!" somebody yelled.

There were more shots. Then the screaming began, and I felt a terrible pressure in my chest. Back, back, back we were pushed. And suddenly, I realized why. Tanks had entered the Boulevard, and were moving forward slowly, trying to get the crowd to disperse. But there were too many people; it was impossible to escape, even if you wanted to.

I heard the cracking sound of breaking glass, then more screams. Night was falling fast; you could hardly see what was going on. People were panicking, being pushed back through windows, being crushed. Bodies tore at me, dragging me this way and that.

"Alys!" I screamed, feeling her fingers slip out of mine.

"Stay strong! Stand your ground," yelled a voice in my ear. I tried to turn round, only thinking about Alys.

"*Alys!*" I yelled again.

But the crowd had carried her away.

ELEVEN

I remember only the blackness, a sort of red-rimmed nothingness into which I was falling, an echo of roaring all around me, gradually fading, fading...

Then nothing.

Until, wavering, then slowly coming into focus, a shadowy face was looking down at me. I ached all over. When I heard that distant, dull roaring again I began to tremble. "It's OK... *Shhh*," said a voice.

I blinked, trying to make out the person's features. But it was too dark.

"Who are you?" I whispered.

"Radu," he said, helping me as I struggled to sit up.

As my eyes got used to the darkness I recognized him. A jaunty peaked cap still on his head, it was the friendly boy whose vantage point we had shared in Palace Square.

"What happened? Where's Alys?" I cried, remembering.

"You were knocked down. I was just behind you and saw it all. Your friend got pushed out of my reach, then somebody by you fell over and hit you on the head with the end of a banner. It was chaos."

"How did we get here?" I asked, looking around. We seemed to be in the side entrance to a building off a narrow alleyway.

"I picked you up," he said. I could see his teeth gleam in a grin. "Didn't know I was that strong!"

"I've got to find Alys. She might be hurt."

"Hey, listen, kid. You haven't got a chance in hell. People are being shot at out there! They won't give in that easily. You've got to stay here – keep out of it."

He put a warning hand on my arm, but I shook it off angrily. "I can't just hide! I've got to try to find her... Please help me!"

"Oh, Lord," muttered Radu, sweeping his hat off and wiping his face, before returning it to his head.

I stood up shakily. "Look," I said, "I'm really grateful to you. You probably saved my life. But you don't have to come with me. I'll look after myself."

He stood up too, towering over me. "How old

are you?" he asked. I told him. "Same age as my sister," he said, "but she's at home – where you should be." Then he sighed. "OK – come on. But keep right behind me all the time, or you'll be in trouble!"

"Who from? Securitate?" I said.

"Very funny…"

When we reached the end of the narrow street, the Boulevard in front of us was like a scene in Hell. I saw people stagger by with blood pouring from wounds in their heads. Others still packed the streets, as if defying the soldiers to sweep them away. There was nobody in charge – how could there be – and yet it seemed that some invisible will made all these people act together, knowing what they must do. Smoke poured from a smouldering car. In the distance was the rat-tat-tat of gunfire. Yet still the crowd stayed. And always there were the voices raised in excitement and fear shouting encouragement to each other.

"Keep steady, keep steady…"

"Link arms, or else we'll fall…"

"Stay! Don't go home!"

"We won't leave! We won't leave!"

"We're free! And we'll stay free! Don't give in!"

Radu held my arm tightly. His face was lit with a rosy light from the scene; his eyes shone. "Look at that, kiddo," he said. "Do you know what that means?" I looked up at him, saying nothing. "It means it's over, that's what it means. It's over for THEM. We've found our voices at last."

I saw a tear find its slow way through the dirt on his face. He didn't bother to wipe it away.

Still holding on to my arm, with a grip so strong it almost hurt, Radu started forward. It was like walking into a whirlpool, as people made sudden lurches to one side or another. But he was determined, and we plunged into the crowd. "We'll start over there, where I pulled you out," he shouted. "And then head in the direction she went. If we can…"

We struggled through. The thought of Alys being lost somewhere in that heaving mass of people, maybe even being hurt, was the only thing that gave me strength. I thought of how she had saved my father, and wanted to cry with the fear of not finding her.

Suddenly a voice shouted his name, and Radu stopped, panting. He'd met a friend in the crowd; I recognized the tall red-haired youth who hadn't wanted us to climb up with them.

"What you doing, Radu? Come on – we're going to pack University Square," he said.

"Have you seen the girl, the tall blonde one,

who was with this one in Palace Square? She's got lost," Radu asked.

"Jesus! Kids shouldn't be out in this!" was the reply.

"I can't leave her on her own," said Radu.

"Listen, I think I did see a girl ... over there, near the line."

He jerked a thumb in the direction of the line of soldiers who stood without moving, but threatening. It was just possible to see their green uniforms, and the tips of their weapons, through the crowd.

"If they started to fire..." muttered Radu. And without saying goodbye to his friend, he dragged me off.

Slowly, slowly, we pushed a way through the crowd. Although people were afraid, there was a giddy atmosphere of celebration too – mad, and holiday-like. Yet the sight of blood, and the odd sound of gunfire, and the knowledge that soon it must get worse, all paralysed me. If it wasn't for Radu I don't think I could have moved. Two names drummed a tattoo in my brain: *Alys ... Mama ... Alys ... Mama ... Alys...*

It would be good to be able to say that I felt brave, that I was proud to be part of this uprising, that my heart swelled with freedom. All that. But it's not true. All I longed to do was find my friend and go home to Mama – and have her put her arms around me so I should feel safe.

Radu was pulling me by my right arm. I put my left hand on top of his hand, to make sure it stayed there, so great was my fear of him being swept away, leaving me alone once more. A perfect stranger, yet already I depended on him.

Suddenly everything happened at once. Somewhere to our right, people started to scream. Radu turned wildly, swore under his breath, and yelled at me to stay with him. I looked. A tank was crawling along, pushing the people back once more. Somebody had stuck a bunch of flowers in the huge gun and I remember wondering, in all the uproar, where on earth they had come from. And all around us people swirled and pushed, trying to get away, caught between the tank's progress and the line of soldiers.

It was then that I glimpsed the back of a blonde head, and a person who suddenly looked very small, jerked hither and thither like a puppet.

"Alys!" I yelled, "ALYS!"

I stretched out a hand through the mass of bodies, but couldn't reach. My voice was drowned by screams. Her head disappeared from my view. She was being carried towards the tank...

"ALYS!" I yelled again. "She's there, Radu, there!"

"Hold on to my jacket," he panted, letting go of my arm and fighting his way through. Like a little animal to its mother I clung on, terrified of letting go. I was blinded by smoke, deafened by shouts, numbed by all the buffeting and blows my body had suffered. Still, Alys was like a beacon. I knew we had to reach her. We would reach her.

Radu's back was ahead of me. Once or twice my fingers felt as if they would slip from the fabric of his jacket as we struggled on. I shut my eyes. Then there was a sort of flurry ahead, and a cry of panic, as he grabbed somebody from behind.

"*Let … go … of … me, you … pig!*" a voice cried, hysterically.

"Stop it!" Radu yelled, trying to grab flailing arms. Then he made a last, strong pull…

And, dirty and dishevelled, Alys was there – all ready to punch him in the eye if she had the chance.

"What? Oh, Flora!" We both burst into tears and fell into each other's arms. "Let's get you out of here," said Radu, dragging us both by a hand.

I don't know how we did it, but somehow we managed to pick a way through the chaos, and collapse in a heap in a doorway.

"I thought I was being arrested," Alys explained, her chest heaving.

Out of breath too, I just nodded weakly, barely able to believe that we were together again. Radu stood watching us, his arms folded. Once he flinched at the sound of gunfire, and glanced over his shoulder.

"Who are you?" asked Alys, staring at her rescuer.

"A student – but never mind all that," he began.

"He's Radu," I said. "He saved me."

"And me," she said.

"I said never mind all that," Radu said, unable to stop the small smile that lit up his face. "But if you want to be my friends, if you want to pay me back, you'll do something for me now. OK?" We nodded, still panting. "I want you to go home. This is going to get really bad. People will be killed tonight, I'm telling you. And I want you out of it – OK?"

Alys and I looked at each other. I half expected her to protest, but instead she nodded. My knees felt weak with relief. I just wanted to go home.

"I'll get you away from the crowds, then you're on your own," said Radu. "Where do you live?"

We told him, and he nodded. "Well, you might find a bus – otherwise you'll have to walk. But promise me you'll go home?"

"I've had enough," said Alys. "But I'm so scared for my parents. They're somewhere in all that." She nodded in the direction of the noise.

"They'll be all right," I said.

"Course they will," said Radu, "Now come on. I'm getting you out of here."

"What about you?" I asked.

"I'll head back to University Square, and stay there. They won't shift us. They can bring the whole damn army."

"Be careful," I said.

He grinned, as if he was about to make a joke, but then his face grew serious. "Listen, kids," he said with a wobble in his voice, "what you've seen tonight is history. You understand? Change at last! No more dictators! I feel as if nothing can stop us now – and that's why I don't care what happens to me. I'd die happily now, if I thought this country would be free, for kids like you and my sister. You hear me? None of us are cowards any more! We'll shout freedom from the rooftops, even if they shoot us down!"

TWELVE

I don't really remember much of that long walk home – only that Alys and I did not let go of each other's arms. If we had, one of us would have fallen.

We passed crowds of people in the streets, all heading for the city centre, because they had seen the rally on television, and were heading to join the revolution. Sometimes in the distance we would hear yelled slogans:

> Olé, olé, olé!
> Ceauşescu's gone away!

It was like walking through a dream.

But our aching legs were real enough, and so was the scattered sound of gunfire. I wondered what my mother would have heard: we had no television, so it was possible she had no knowledge of what had happened. In any case, she would be desperately worried. Alys was wondering if her parents would be at home, or still caught up in the violence we had left behind.

Instead of going home, I climbed the stairs with her to their apartment. All was dark and silent. Alys chewed her lips, then said resolutely, "I know they'll be all right."

"Come home with me to Mama," I said gently. I knew Alys and I had to look after each other from now on. Nothing would change that, not after what we'd been through. So, arm in arm, we walked down again, and crossed over to my block. As we climbed wearily upstairs, my heart started thumping wildly at the thought of seeing Mama.

My mother fell on my neck as if she were drowning, and I was a passing log. Then she cried, and I felt more guilty than ever before in my life. Except when I learned about Daniel Ghiban...

She had heard the sound of shooting in the distance, searched for me around the area, and been told that "something had happened'. That's all. Frantic, she had gone to the Grosus' flat, to find nobody there. Then a neighbour of theirs told her I had been seen heading off with Alys.

"I knew then," she said, "that you two had gone

to the centre. I was frantic..."

"It was my fault. I'm sorry, Mrs Popescu," said Alys, hanging her head.

Mama looked at us. We must have been a pathetic sight – filthy and exhausted. "I'm going to put you both in the big bed. You need to sleep," she said decisively.

"What about my parents?" wailed Alys, suddenly, sounding like a little girl.

"Once I've settled you I'll walk over and put a note under your door," said Mama.

We slept for twelve hours. When we woke up, it was to the sound of voices. My mother and Alys's parents were sitting at the table drinking tea. Alys leapt up; there was a great fuss of reunion and explanation and general delight.

Then Mr Grosu got up. "I'm going back," he said.

"Why, Tata?" asked Alys, reaching out a hand.

"Don't go," said Mrs Grosu.

He stood, looking down at us all, his face a mixture of seriousness and excitement. "Listen," he said, "I saw people killed. I saw a teenage boy dying in the arms of his friend."

I closed my eyes when he said that, briefly imagining Radu. *Please let him be all right, please let him be all right.*

Mr Grosu was still speaking. "And it's getting worse. Ceauşescu and his lot aren't giving up without a fight – and I've got to be there." He looked at my mother, and added quietly, "Constantin would feel the same."

"I know," she said. "If only he'd stayed."

"Maybe he did," I said.

She shook her head. "No; I'm sure he crossed the border... What a thing! To risk your life that way, when just a short time afterwards everything would change."

"Don't let's speak too soon," said Mrs Grosu. "We don't know what's going to happen."

"I'll tell you one thing," said Alys's father, heading for the door, "Ceauşescu's finished. Of that I'm sure."

He was right. Three days later, on Christmas Day, Nicolae Ceauşescu and his wife were put to death by a firing squad. But they had told their followers to fight to the last man, so the shooting went on, all through the city now. We even heard gunfire near our block. There were hidden snipers everywhere. Four days ... five days, and all the time we were like prisoners in the block. And all the time, Alys's father did not return.

The morning came when Mama and I had

nothing to eat in the flat, except for a half-full jar of pickled gherkins. It was quiet outside, a bright, cold, frosty day, so we decided that we had to go out to find some food. I had grown used to my stomach rumbling; my foolish dreams about luxuries like chocolate and bananas seemed a long time ago.

So we set out, arm in arm, each carrying a shopping bag, and planning our expedition with all the expertise of military commanders. We decided that we would split up when we reached the local shops – Mama joining the most promising queue, whilst I scoured the side streets where the country people would sit selling their wares, if you were lucky. Then I'd go back to her, and she'd direct me to the next queue.

After I'd left her I set off at a run determined I would make my mother a good meal. Since my father disappeared, I felt much more protective towards her, and I looked back with some contempt at the little girl who only thought of herself. Mama was still frail; it was as if she would only recover her full strength when she heard from my father.

If she heard from my father.

I couldn't waste time brooding on such things; ahead of me a little crowd of people clustered around someone sitting on the pavement. I recognized many of them: people we used to see every day, but not speak to. I joined them. It was hard to see, but at last between backs and elbows I glimpsed an old man, wearing his conical peasant hat; a sack spread on the ground before him, on it a tumble of vegetables. He had a couple of sacks behind him, so there was clearly a good supply of turnips, swedes and cabbages.

What's more, everybody was talking – stranger to stranger.

"I'm glad they were killed."

"I'd have killed them myself."

"I heard there's already thirty free newspapers on the streets."

"Who cares about newspapers? It's fruit I want!"

There was an easy, friendly, uncompetitive atmosphere – like I had never known. I looked around. Further up the street people were crowded round some sort of poster on a wall, reading it and exchanging views. Everything was buzzing – as if a whole nation, asleep for centuries, had suddenly woken up.

I waited patiently in the ragged queue, and at last came to the front, buying eight potatoes, one huge turnip, two smaller swedes, a good cabbage, and four onions. They filled my bag. I wanted to leap and yell for joy. But I decided I wouldn't give in to the temptation to rush to show my mother. There might be some more goodies on sale further along.

Turning quickly in my eagerness, grinning with pleasure, I bumped into somebody who had just arrived to see what was for sale. My shoulder cannoned into a chest. I nearly dropped my precious bag. I didn't look up, just mumbled an apology, when I heard a sharp intake of breath that had nothing to do with the collision.

I looked up, and found myself face to face with Daniel Ghiban. For a few seconds I was incapable of movement or speech, and so was he. We stood staring at each other, whilst the life of the street moved all around us, as if we were not there. Daniel looked terrible. His handsome face was pitted with shadows; his eyes were bloodshot and gazed at me from dark craters in his face.

"You!" I said.

"I came out to get some food," he explained.

"Me too," I said.

This is ridiculous, I thought, *we're talking as if nothing has happened.*

I made a slight movement, as if to go on my way. Daniel made an equally slight movement with one hand, as if he was going to detain me, then he let it drop. And his gaze slid down to the pavement. That decided me. Why should he be allowed to escape like that?

"Look at me," I said.

He did so, and once again I was shocked by his appearance. He was a remnant of the person he had been.

"I have to ask you. Why did you do those things?" I spoke coldly, wondering why I didn't hit him.

He shook his head.

"I need to know," I insisted. "I trusted you. And look what happened. Do you realize what you did?"

"I couldn't help it!" he burst out. "I had no choice. I was just doing what I'd been taught to do."

"And did that make it all right?" I sneered.

"No."

"I hope you suffer. I really hope you suffer," I said.

He looked as if he was about to cry, and I could hardly catch the next words.

"I'm already suffering," he muttered.

"What's happened to you?"

"My father ... my fa-ther ... he..."

Inside I already knew what he was going to say.

His head was bent, and his chest heaved for a few seconds as he fought for control. Then he went on: "My father was killed – shot – two days ago. He was on duty, and he ... didn't come back. Then some people came to our door, laughing. They threw his coat at my mother. It was all covered with blood. They said he got what he ... deserved..." He swallowed, then went on, "My mother doesn't know what we'll do. We have to get away, but I don't know where we can go."

He couldn't go on. I saw a tear run down his cheek. All my instincts told me to put out a hand to try to comfort him, but of course, I couldn't. Those people were right. His father, a hated Securitate man, did deserve whatever he got. This was a war – the old order against the new. But...

The boy who stood before me was still a person, still a son mourning for his father. I suppose your father is your father whatever he's done.

And so would I obey my father, even if he told me to betray people? Would I think it right just because he said so?

The thought of Tata brought all the memories sharply back, and immediately, hate for Daniel threatened to drive out the other things I was feeling. Then he looked up at me, with those exhausted, brimming eyes, and said, "I'm so sorry."

It was very quiet – and hopeless, too. "I'm sorry."

I knew I would never see him again – that I didn't want to see him again. But it was impossible not to feel sorry for Daniel Ghiban. Without his smart clothes, and chewing gum, and chocolate, he was nothing. Without his father he was nothing. He was in a dark pit, and I was standing in the light, looking down on him. And feeling – pity.

"Flora," he said, as if asking me to make a response.

I looked at him for a long time. Then I said quietly, "I believe you. I believe you're sorry."

"Can you ... will you ... forgive me?" he asked.

In the second before I replied two armies fought out their own battle within me. I put my hand up to my neck and fingered my birthday scarf, then let my eyes travel all over this shabby, broken boy who stood there, his eyes pleading with me.

"Yes," I said, "I do forgive you."

Then I turned my back and walked away, in case I should change my mind.

As I walked up the street I found myself shaking, and near to tears. But there was little time to think about Daniel Ghiban. For I saw Alys and my mother running towards me, shouting my name at the top of their voices, so that people turned to look. Mama's cotton headscarf had slipped back, so that her dark hair streamed out. Her face was rosy with cold and excitement. As they reached me I expected Mama to tell me that she had found some meat, or some other such piece of good luck.

"Flora!" she panted. "Alys just came to find me. You'll never guess – Tata's been seen! He was fighting in the city centre. Tata's still in Bucharest!"

Then she flung her arms around me, and started to cry, not caring about the stares of passers-by.

"My father came home. He's been occupying the radio and television studios," said Alys, "and one of his group said they'd seen Constantin Popescu in the fight at University Square."

"Oh, Flora!" Mama sobbed, "I so want to see him."

"Come on, then," I said briskly.

"Where?"

"Well, we'll have to go and find him," I said.

"I'll come too," said Alys impetuously, but I shook my head.

"No – you should stay with your parents, Alys. This is for me and Mama to do by ourselves."

The buses were running again, although the journey to the city centre was far from normal. There was the odd sound of a sniper; and smoke came from half burnt-out buildings. There were still crowds on the streets. It was easy to pick up all the news from the conversation of people around – because that was the most amazing thing, which stands out almost above everything else. The way people talked. Their gags off at last, they were unstoppable. Silence had found its voice, and would not be shut up.

So we knew that the army had blazed away, that many people had been killed, that tear gas had filled University Square, but the demonstrators had not budged. Even when the Ceauşescus had been executed, the killings had gone on. Nobody was in charge. Both sides had weapons.

It had not occurred to me that finding one man in the centre of Bucharest, whilst the revolution was still going on, was an impossibility. When Mama and I started to wander through the streets I knew we would find him. We had to find him. And so I took her arm, and encouraged her, and never let her give up hope.

The city seemed stunned, like a huge animal, licking its wounds after a fight. Palace Square was still wreathed in smoke, some of the buildings half-destroyed, rubbish everywhere. Tanks were parked here and there, but they weren't moving, still less firing. On the contrary, we saw a crowd of women go up to one tank, and hand up bread and flowers to the soldiers. "You're with us now!" they called, and the men smiled, receiving the gifts.

My mother looked at me in disbelief. You see, when you have lived your whole life in fear of men in uniform, sights like this were miraculous. Not surprising that I thought that anything was possible – any miracle. Even finding Tata.

Everywhere there were shrines. In the gloom of the winter day, the tail-end of the year, the thin yellow candles stuck in pieces of wood, glowed like tiny beacons of hope. Here and there we saw people sitting and crying quietly near by, some-times repeating one name over and over again.

The names of the dead.

Hours passed. We had no method. All we could do was to go up to groups of men who had clearly been involved in the fighting and ask, over and over again, "Do you know Constantin Popescu? Have you heard the name Constantin Popescu?" Always they shook their heads. Sometimes they looked at each other as if to say we were mad.

We saw foreigners with television cameras, film-ing the aftermath of the revolution. I heard American accents, and German, and French, and stared at these people in wonderment. They were so well-dressed, the Westerners, in big smart coats, all confident. Crowds of little kids hung around them, begging for gum and chocolate. They got it, too. But I wasn't interested in such things.

My mother turned to me, as we huddled at the side of Boulevard Magheru, resting for a while. "We'll never find him, Flora," she said wearily.

"We will! I know it!" I cried.

Just then there was noise further up the street – a shouting and scuffling, then the sound of a single shot. Mama and I flung ourselves flat on the cold ground, and did not dare to move for about five minutes. Then, carefully, we raised our heads.

About a hundred metres away someone was lying on the pavement, with two or three people gathered round. We could hear groaning.

"Quickly!" shouted Mama, and we ran to see if we could help, keeping our heads down as we went. As we reached the group she called out, "Let me see! I know about first aid!" in a clear, authoritative voice.

A young man was lying on the ground, groaning loudly, blood pouring from a wound in his head. Three friends knelt by him, pale and scared. My mother knelt too, making a quick examination. Then she looked up, relieved.

"Looks worse than it is. But just half an inch more, and he would be dead. As it is, the bullet just grazed. But we need to stop the bleeding..."

She tore the kerchief from her head, and folded it into a thick pad. This she held firmly against the wound. Then she looked at the three young men. "I need a bandage – something to keep it in place," she said. They looked helpless. They had nothing.

Then I knew what I had to do. My hand flew up and touched my birthday scarf, then fumbled quickly to untie the knot.

"Mama! This will do it!" I said, smoothing it out, and rolling it across so that it made a long strip.

"Good girl! Now I'll hold this in place, and you tie it round – really firmly, mind! You – you hold up his head." She nodded to one of the boys who obeyed; and in a minute the victim was bandaged. Mama helped him to sit up. "That's it – gently. You'll probably feel faint," she murmured gently.

The young man opened his eyes, and I stared at him. I had seen him before, but couldn't remember when. He looked terrible; face dead white, freckles showing up lividly between the streaks of dirt and dried blood. And his carroty hair matted with reddish-black clots...

I remembered at last. He was the boy we'd first met in Palace Square, the one who hadn't wanted us to steal his place, the one who was my student Radu's friend!

"Hey!" I said excitedly. "You were with Radu,

weren't you? Where is he? Is he all right?"

They all stared at me. There was a horrible silence for a few minutes, as the boys looked at each other, then my mother, then back at me. The one who was injured just gave a low groan, and buried his face in his hands. He didn't look up again, just sat moaning softly. One of his friends put an arm around his shoulders and looked at me with a desperately sad face.

"Radu... Radu died," he said simply. "He was shot. We couldn't do anything..."

His voice tailed off. I knelt there, stunned. My mother put out a hand, pulled me up, and let me away. I stopped, and glanced back at the little group, with a picture in my mind of a cheerful, friendly face under a blue peaked cap. But all I could see were four shocked young men, in the bleak street; one of them moaning into his hands, his head bandaged brightly in my precious birthday scarf.

Somebody was selling roasted chestnuts on the street. My mother stopped and bought some, but I shook my head. She insisted, and I took one. It burnt my mouth, and that moment's pain, followed by the delicious taste, brought me back to life.

"Flora…" said Mama.

"Don't let's talk about it," I said. "I just want to think about Tata."

On we went, asking, looking, asking, looking … passing men with guns, breathing in bitter smoke, hearing now the sound of singing, now the sound of weeping. It was like walking through all the levels of Hell in old pictures I had seen, taken from the ancient churches of our country. And I wondered what we had all done, to be punished like this. Yet, I reminded myself, we're free now. Once this bit is over, everything will be all right. As long as we can find Tata…

We reached a patch of green in the centre, a small park where the road split into two. An old woman dressed in black was kneeling there, singing quietly. It sounded like a prayer. A rough cross, just two bits of wood tied together with string, was stuck in the ground, and in front of it she had put two thin yellow candles. As we approached she was in the act of placing a small bunch of flowers and leaves at the foot of the little cross. And all the time she muttered her prayers.

We were just a couple of metres away, when I heard my mother gasp and at the same time she gripped my arm so tightly I thought her fingers would crack my bone.

"Look!" she croaked.

On the rough cross someone had scrawled a name in white chalk. It said CONSTANTIN.

"Mama! There's lots of men called Constantin," I whispered, but she wasn't listening. She knelt down beside the old woman, her face white, and asked her if this shrine was in memory of a relative of hers.

"No, my dear," came the reply. "Just a young man I saw die. I held his head in my hands, I begged him not to die, but I couldn't save him. He just told me his name, that's all. Just his first name… May the Lord have mercy upon him."

"A boy?" asked Mama.

"No, a man. In his thirties, I'd say."

"What … what did he look like?" asked Mama.

"Dark hair, dark eyes … he was a fine-looking man. Not tall…"

"His clothes…?"whispered Mama.

"Oh, I can't remember… So much blood… But – yes – a blue jacket. Too thin for this weather. Poor man, poor man… Dear Lord, save his soul."

I looked into my mother's eyes and knew what she thought. Myself, I refused to believe it. But her mind was made up.

"Where did they take him?" she asked, standing up.

The old woman shook her head, patting the flowers, and murmuring her prayers. But a man standing near overheard, and told Mama that the bodies of the people killed in this area of the city had been taken to a public building near by, which was acting as a temporary morgue.

"Where?" asked my mother. Her voice was firm now, as if she knew she had to be strong, whatever happened. The man pointed, and gave her directions. Mama turned to me. "You can stay here, Flora. It may not be..."

"I'm coming with you, Mama," I said, loudly, and took her arm.

Once we were inside the building I felt less brave. People were walking slowly out, supporting each other, sobbing and wailing because they had found their dead loved ones. In the huge room ahead of us, its double doors thrown open, we could see rows of bodies on the floor, all covered in blankets. Over the door someone had hung the new Romanian flag – red, yellow and black, with a round hole cut out of the middle. Mama moved forward slowly, until she was standing beneath it.

"I don't want you to come in with me, Flora. You must wait here," she said.

I was frozen, incapable of movement. The

170

thought of her walking on alone, lifting all those cloths to search for my father's face ... finding him, without my arm to give her support... It was impossible. And yet I did not want to go on. I was afraid.

And, I realized, even if Tata wasn't there, we might come across the body of Radu. It was unbearable. Yet she would have to bear it. "No," I said at last. "It's just you and me, Mama. Whatever you can look at, I can look at too."

As we took the first steps into the room, holding on to each other for strength, I felt her start to tremble. And the voice in my brain was just saying *Please, please, please, please* ... when the universe stopped its sickening, dizzying whirl. I remember it all in slow motion. The sound of running feet, in the distance it seemed – yet just behind us. And a voice a million miles away, shouting, "Rodika! Rodika! Flora!" Echoing, yet right in my ear. And my mother turning round stiffly, like someone in a dream, to confront the man behind us. The man who was lurching towards us, his head bandaged, a gun slung over his shoulder, his blue jacket torn and bloody, almost unrecognizable, but...

"Constantin!"

"TATA!"

Then he was clutching us both, laughing and

crying at the same time, choking but trying to explain.

"I saw you come in," he said. "I was on duty at the top of the house across the street, looking out for snipers. I couldn't believe it was you!"

"Oh, where've you been? Why didn't you come home?" sobbed my mother.

"It's such a long story," he said, hugging her tightly. "I went underground, then I knew the revolution was going to start, and it wouldn't have been safe for me to have come home. Since then..." He shrugged, and touched his bandaged head. "I was out of action for a couple of days with this, then it was back to the fight. Everybody was needed. But I knew the time was coming when I could come and see you. I couldn't wait..."

"She thought you were dead," I whispered, finding his hand and clinging to it. In front of us someone was crying, and it seemed almost wrong to be so lucky, so happy.

"Not me! I'm more alive than ever," cried Tata, turning us round, and walking us out of that sad building, his arms around our shoulders, our arms around his waist.

"It's over now," he said, "and we can all start again. A new life, Flora!"

I gazed up at him, hardly able to see, my heart

thumping like mad. Behind his back, I clutched my mother's hand, so that we were like a little wall, which nothing could break down – no politics, no presidents. Just the three of us against the world.

"Let's go home now," I said.

AUTHOR'S NOTE

An old Romanian proverb says, "A change of rulers is the joy of fools" – meaning that getting rid of one regime will not make for a miracle. Old ways do not disappear overnight.

In March 1990 I went to Romania to research a novel for adults called *Lost Footsteps*. This was just after the events of *The Voices of Silence* had happened, and there were still candles in the streets to mark where people had been killed. Later that year I went back and drove all over the country. Both trips made a deep impression on me, which is why I ended up writing two novels, a short story and a screenplay – all set in Romania.

Although the "revolution" my Flora witnessed was over, things hadn't improved as much as people had hoped. Of course, the regime of the dictator had been overthrown, and there was more free-dom. The West was beginning to invest in the country; there was a general sense of opening up. But people still waited in line for basic things like bread and meat, and the longed-for rise in the standard of living had not come about.

To make it worse, there was corruption

everywhere, just like before. Aid workers from Britain, France, Canada and the USA who went to help the orphans were shocked when toys, clothes and medicines donated by generous people back home just vanished, then reappeared on the market – for a price. They were depressed that some Romanians did not seem able, or willing, to help themselves. But the people had been poor and oppressed for centuries, not just years, and ways of thinking and acting can become engrained.

Does that mean change is impossible? Of course not. When countries like Poland, Czechoslovakia and Romania finally rejected the communism of Soviet Russia, history was changed; and history is, after all, nothing more or less than the lives of individual men, women and children. Brave people have always stood up to their oppressors in the end – and always will. That's why we must have hope.

Now Romania is a part of the European Union, which means that many Romanians have come to Britain looking for a better life. This tells us there must still be much poverty at home; Romania (so beautiful in parts) is still not prosperous. The sad truth is, most thirteen-year-old Romanian girls today would still think of a scarf as a special gift.

Bel Mooney, 2007

Amnesty International

The Voices of Silence is a work of fiction, but its description of the Romanian Revolution depicts fear and violence that is still real in many countries today. Not being able to speak freely because of fear of the consequences can lead to mistrust and emnity among friends and families. Life under a repressive regime is highly restrictive, denying people their basic human rights.

Human rights are the principles that allow individuals freedom to live dignified lives, free from abuse, fear and want and free to express their own beliefs. Human rights belong to all of us, regardless of who we are or where we live.

Amnesty International is a movement of ordinary people from across the world standing up for humanity and human rights. Our purpose is to protect individuals wherever justice, fairness, freedom and truth are denied.

Youth Groups
We have an active membership of over 550 youth groups. Youth groups are gatherings of young people in schools, sixth-form colleges or youth clubs who meet to learn about and campaign for Amnesty International. You can also join as an individual member and receive magazines to keep you up to date about ways you can help us. If you would like to join Amnesty International or set up a youth group, or simply find out more, please telephone our Education and Student Team on 020 7033 1596, email student@amnesty.org.uk or visit www.amnesty.org.uk/education/youthandstudent/.

Amnesty International UK, The Human Rights Action Centre,
17–25 New Inn Yard, London EC2A 3EA. Tel: 020 7033 1500.

www.amnesty.org.uk

All royalties from the sale of this book will go to the work of Amnesty International UK.